Holiday Magic

Look for more

titles:

1 It's a Twin Thing
2 How to Flunk Your First Date
3 The Sleepover Secret
4 One Twin Too Many
5 To Snoop or Not to Snoop
6 My Sister the Supermodel
7 Two's a Crowd
8 Let's Party
9 Calling All Boys
10 Winner Take All
11 P.S. Wish You Were Here
12 The Cool Club
13 War of the Wardrobes
14 Bye-Bye Boyfriend
15 It's Snow Problem
16 Likes Me, Likes Me Not
17 Shore Thing
18 Two for the Road
19 Surprise, Surprise!
20 Sealed with a Kiss
21 Now You See Him, Now You Don't
22 April Fools' Rules!
23 Island Girls
24 Surf, Sand, and Secrets
25 Closer Than Ever
26 The Perfect Gift
27 The Facts About Flirting
28 The Dream Date Debate
29 Love-Set-Match
30 Making a Splash
31 Dare to Scare
32 Santa Girls
33 Heart to Heart
34 Prom Princess
35 Camp Rock 'n' Roll
36 Twist and Shout
37 Hocus-pocus

Holiday Magic

by Diana G. Gallagher

from the series created by Robert Griffard
& Howard Adler

HarperCollins*Entertainment*
An Imprint of HarperCollins*Publishers*

A PARACHUTE PRESS BOOK

A PARACHUTE PRESS BOOK
Parachute Publishing, L.L.C.
156 Fifth Avenue
Suite 325
NEW YORK
NY 10010

First published in the USA by Harper*Entertainment* 2004
First published in Great Britain by HarperCollins*Entertainment* 2005
HarperCollins*Entertainment* is an imprint of HarperCollins*Publishers* Ltd,
77 - 85 Fulham Palace Road, Hammersmith, London W6 8JB

TWO OF A KIND books created and produced by
Parachute Publishing, L.C.C. in cooperation with Dualstar Publications,
a division of Dualstar Entertainment Group, Inc.

The HarperCollins children's website address is
www.harpercollinschildrensbooks.co.uk

1 3 5 7 9 10 8 6 4 2

ISBN 0 00 720482 5

Printed and bound in Great Britain by Clays Ltd, St Ives plc

Chapter 1

Friday

Dear Diary,

I have never, ever had a brownie that tasted as amazing as the one I had today. My new friend, Brigitte Jardin, brought me one for lunch. I shouldn't have been surprised by how good it was.

Brigitte's mom made the brownies, and Brigitte's mom is Monique Jardin. She's a world-famous French chef. She sent Brigitte a whole box of goodies.

You know how much I like to cook, Right, Diary? Maybe I can exchange recipes with Monique Jardin someday! Why not? Brigitte and I have been hanging out since she came to White Oak Academy for Girls two weeks ago all the way from France.

"That brownie was so good, Brigitte!" I said and grinned. "My stomach is growling!"

Brigitte gasped. "Why? Did it make you sick?"

"Not at all, it just made me hungry for more," I explained.

"Oh," Brigitte said. She smoothed back her short dark hair. Her blue eyes looked troubled. "Sometimes American expressions confuse me."

I keep forgetting that Brigitte is a long way from home. New Hampshire must be very different from

France. Her mother wanted her to learn about America. That's why she sent Brigitte to attend White Oak Academy for the rest of the year.

"Can I sit here, too?" Phoebe Cahill, my roommate, stopped at the end of the table.

"Sure," I said as Phoebe sat down.

I smiled. This was a great chance for Brigitte to get friendly with someone else. She's having a little trouble fitting in – mostly because she's very shy. She thinks her English isn't good enough. The truth is, Brigitte speaks English almost as well as I do.

Brigitte and I sit next to each other in history class. She broke her pencil the first day, and I loaned her one of mine. That was two weeks ago. We've been friends ever since.

"Hi, Brigitte," Phoebe said. "How's everything going?"

"Fine," Brigitte mumbled. She glanced up with a tight smile. Then she looked back at her tray.

Brigitte will never make friends that way, I thought. "Why are you so late for lunch, Phoebe?" I asked.

"I've got an experiment going on in biology lab," Phoebe explained. "I have to be back in fifteen minutes. What did I miss?"

"Only the best brownies in the whole world," I said. "Brigitte's mom sent them all the way from *France*."

"Wow! Really? My mom *buys* brownies at the bakery. She's the worst cook." Phoebe grinned. "She can't even make brownies from a mix."

"I bet you'd love Monique Jardin's brownies," I said. "You can try one. I have more in my room."

Mrs. Pritchard, the headmistress, walked to the front of the dining hall and clapped her hands for attention.

"What's going on?" Phoebe asked.

I shrugged. I didn't have a clue.

"Quiet, please!" Mrs. Pritchard waited until everyone stopped talking. "This year the whole school will participate in different projects for the White Oak Winter Festival. Each First Form dorm will run a restaurant."

"A real restaurant?" Phoebe said.

"I guess so," I said. "It sounds like fun."

"Running a restaurant is a lot of work," Brigitte said.

Mrs. Pritchard glanced at our table. We stopped talking to listen as the headmistress explained the rules.

"Every dorm will have a budget," Mrs. Pritchard said. "You can use it to buy food, decorations – whatever you choose. But you can't go over that amount.

"Each restaurant must get at least twenty reservations," Mrs. Pritchard added. "Your customers can be students from White Oak or Harrington Academy – teachers, staff, or visitors. The price of each meal will be eight dollars."

"I know exactly what Phipps House can do!" Dana Woletsky said. She was sitting at the next table with her friends, Kristen Lindquist and Brooke Miller. Dana lived in Phipps, but Kristen and Brooke lived in Porter House with me. I avoid Dana as much as possible. Dana likes to make life difficult for me and my sister, Mary-Kate.

Mrs. Pritchard smiled. "To make the project a little more exciting, Jerome Dupont will judge each restaurant."

"Who's Jerome Dupont?" Brigitte whispered.

I shrugged. Phoebe raised her hand and asked, "Who's Jerome Dupont?"

"He's the food critic for the town newspaper, the *Gazette*," the headmistress said. "Mr. Dupont will consider the decorations, the menu, and the food. Then he'll award a five-star rating to one dorm."

"Is that good?" Summer Sorenson asked. She was sitting at the next table with Mary-Kate and Campbell Smith, my sister's roommate.

"Five stars is the best," Mary-Kate told her.

"The winning dorm will have an article and a photograph in the *Gazette*," Mrs. Pritchard added.

"Cool!" Phoebe was impressed. "I've never had my picture in a real newspaper before."

"And as an extra-special treat," Mrs. Pritchard finished, "the winning dorm will get a pizza party at Champs."

Everyone clapped and cheered. Champs has great pizza and arcade games. It's everyone's favorite hangout.

"Every dorm will have a meeting after classes this afternoon," Mrs. Pritchard explained. "You have to decide what kind of restaurant your dorm will create and which jobs everyone will do."

Phoebe stood up. "Yikes! I've got to get back to my experiment. I'm trying to see if I can get a plant to grow with only fifteen minutes of light a day. If I don't get back, my whole project will be ruined!"

"We'll see you at Porter House later," I said.

"Is Champs good?" Brigitte asked after Phoebe walked away.

"It's great!" I said. "I hope we win. It's my dream to be a chef – and now I get to practise in our very own restaurant."

"You can't win against Phipps House, Ashley," Dana said. She stood up with her tray. "Jerome

Dupont is going to give us his five-star rating."

I motioned Brigitte to lean closer. I didn't want Dana to overhear. "Ignore her," I said softly. "I have the perfect recipe for the contest. My mom won a blue ribbon for it once. She even had *her* picture in a Chicago newspaper."

"She did?" Brigitte's eyes got wide. "What did she make?"

"Chicken potpie," I said.

"Is that an American dish?" Brigitte asked.

"Yes," I said. "It's a pie made with chicken and vegetables in gravy."

Dana stopped behind my chair. "If you're making potpies, my dorm will win – no question!"

Summer wrinkled her nose. "Who's making potpies?" she asked. "They're so – ordinary."

That's when I realized I might have a problem, Diary. Chicken potpie doesn't *sound* very exciting.

How can I convince everyone at Porter House that Jerome Dupont will love my mom's Chunky Chicken Under Cover?

Dear Diary,

Guess what Porter House will be for the White Oak Winter Festival? A restaurant! With reservations and waitresses and everything.

I know what you're thinking, Diary. I hate to cook. A lot! But I don't have to worry about that. Ashley is the best cook in the First Form, and she *wants* to be the chef. That's all she talked about when we walked back to Porter House after classes.

But for Ashley it's not just about cooking, Diary. Our mother died years ago. Making her recipes is one way Ashley remembers her.

Ashley loved to watch our mom cook. And Mom would always let her help. They would roll out the dough for Mom's special potpies together and I would watch. I just loved eating Chunky Chicken Under Cover! It was our favorite.

"What if no one wants our restaurant to make chicken potpie?" Ashley asked me. She looked worried. "Then they won't vote for me to be the chef."

"I'm sure everyone in our dorm will vote for you at the project meeting, Ashley," I said.

Ashley went upstairs to her room, and I went to the lounge with Campbell.

"Don't you think running a restaurant will be hard?" Campbell asked. We sat down on the floor in the lounge. All the sofas and chairs were full.

"Not really," I said.

Miss Viola, our housemother, started the meeting. "There's a lot to do to run a restaurant. But each girl will only have one job. I'll be here to help if you have a problem. Mrs. Pritchard wants the students to do everything, even run the meetings." Miss Viola gave Summer Sorenson a list of jobs.

Summer stood by the fireplace. "Is everyone here?" she asked, counting heads. Most of the time she just goes along with what everyone else wants to do. Today she was taking charge.

"Sorry we're late!" Ashley said, dashing in with her new friend, Brigitte. They sat down near Campbell and me.

"Does anyone mind if I'm the hostess?" Summer asked. "I just love dressing up, and I can write down reservations."

"It's okay with me," Elise Van Hook said. "We need someone with a great smile to greet people."

"What about Ashley as hostess?" Lavender Duncan asked.

"No, thanks," Ashley said. "I really don't want that job."

I smiled. I knew Ashley was holding out for chef.

"Who wants Summer to be hostess?" Phoebe asked. She raised her hand.

Everyone voted to make Summer the hostess. Then Summer checked her list of jobs. "Now we need to choose a head waitress."

"Mary-Kate would be great!" Campbell said, pointing at me.

"Ashley could do that job, too," Lavender said.

"I don't want that job, either," Ashley said. She shook her head. "Let Mary-Kate do it."

Everybody voted for me to be the head waitress.

"I think Elise should be in charge of decorations," Summer said.

Lavender started to mention Ashley, but Ashley quickly shook her head.

"Does anyone want to make flyers?" Summer asked. "And put them up around campus?"

Jolene Dupree, Kristen, and Brooke raised their hands, and we all voted for them. All the main jobs were taken, except for the chef. Everyone else would be kitchen helpers, waitresses, or decorators.

"Do you want to cook, Ashley?" Lavender asked.

"I'd love to!" Ashley said and raised her hand.

I looked around the room. Nobody else volunteered, so we didn't have to vote.

Then Ashley stood up. "I have an announcement," she began. "Brigitte's mother sent her a box of treats. And she wants to share them with everyone."

"Great!" Cheryl Miller exclaimed. "I'm starved."

Brigitte blushed but didn't say anything. She

took the top off a pink pastry box. Then she handed the box to Cheryl.

Cheryl took a white cookie out of the box. It had a gooey red center. "What is this?" she asked.

"A Raspberry Snowdrop," Brigitte said.

Phoebe took the box from Cheryl. "They look delicious."

Everyone ooohed and aaahed as they passed the box around. The cookies had a sweet-tangy flavor.

"I've had these before!" Kristen said, pointing to the silver writing on the box. "When I was in Paris. This is Monique Jardin's signature!"

"That's my mother's logo," Brigitte said quietly.

"Monique Jardin is your *mother*, Brigitte?" Brooke's eyes got wide. "*The* Monique Jardin? The famous French chef?"

Brigitte nodded.

Summer blinked. "My mother watches the Monique Jardin TV show every day!"

"My mom has three of her cookbooks," Jolene said. "And a whole set of Monique Jardin baking pans."

"She has her own line of cookware, too?" Kristen asked, biting into the cookie. She closed her eyes to chew. "Awesome!"

"I told you they'd love the cookies, Brigitte," Ashley said.

Brigitte just nodded, but she was smiling.

"Maybe we should serve fantastic French stuff at our holiday restaurant," Elise said. "I bet Jerome Dupont *loves* gourmet French food."

"Or we could just serve desserts," Cheryl suggested. "That would be different."

"It might work," Kristen agreed. "Especially if Brigitte is our chef."

I heard Ashley gasp behind me. No one else noticed, but I knew how much my sister wanted to be the chef.

"Brigitte *has* to be our chef," Brooke said. "Then we'll win Mr. Dupont's five-star rating for sure. You can make desserts, right, Brigitte?"

"Well . . . sure," Brigitte said and smiled at all the girls smiling at her.

"Let's vote," Kristen said. "Everyone who wants Brigitte – "

"Wait!" I jumped to my feet.

"What is it, Mary-Kate?" Brooke asked, annoyed.

"Ashley really wants to be chef," I said.

"And Ashley is a really good cook, too," Phoebe added.

"And she wants to make one of our mother's best recipes," I said. "Chunky Chicken Under Cover won first prize in a Chicago cooking contest."

From the corner of my eye I saw Ashley smile. Hey, sisters are supposed to help each other.

"My mom used a secret ingredient," I added. "That's what made her chicken potpie so great!"

"But how can we choose?" Summer asked. "Ashley's my friend and a great cook. But Brigitte grew up with a famous chef."

"Let's have a cook-off tomorrow!" I suggested. "The food will decide."

"Super idea!" Summer stood up again. "Everybody in favor of a cook-off between Brigitte and Ashley tomorrow – "

Every hand went up before Summer finished.

That was one of my better brainstorms, Diary. Now Ashley has a fair chance to be picked for chef.

Just as the meeting ended, a loud crash sounded from the front hall.

"What was that?" Phoebe asked.

"Something broke," Campbell said.

I raced to the doorway. I couldn't believe what I saw. "What are *you* doing here?" I cried.

Dana was kneeling by a potted plant that had fallen off the hall table. She was frantically scooping up dirt and dumping it back into the pot.

Campbell peered over my shoulder. "You ruined our plant, Dana!"

Dana's head snapped up. "I did not."

I wasn't worried about the plant. I was worried that Dana was up to something.

The other girls crowded behind me. They wanted to see what was going on. Campbell, Phoebe, and I moved into the hall. "What are you doing, Dana?" I asked again.

"I, uh – " Dana scooped up the last of the dirt. She put it into the pot and then put the pot back onto the table. "Fixing the plant."

"I meant what are you doing *here*," I said. "At Porter House?"

"Oh. I" – Dana hesitated – "I . . . just came to say 'Hi' to Kristen and Brooke."

Everyone stared at Dana.

"What?" Dana demanded, as though we had been caught dumping plants at Phipps House. "I can't visit my friends?"

Kristen shoved through the crowd to the door. "Hi, Dana! What are you doing here?"

"Is your meeting over? Are you and Brooke ready to go to dinner?" Dana sounded angry.

Kristen looked puzzled. "It's only four-thirty."

"Whatever." Dana threw up her hands and left.

Kristen and Brooke ran after her. They wouldn't

do anything to make Dana mad. They like being in Dana's circle of cool friends.

"That was weird," Campbell said.

"Yeah," I agreed.

Diary, I don't think Dana came to Porter House to see her friends. Everyone knows that Dana Woletsky will do just about anything to get what she wants. And I'm pretty sure Dana wants Phipps House to get Jerome Dupont's five-star rating, a picture in the *Gazette,* and a pizza party.

But I really want my dorm to win, too!

Chapter 2

Saturday

Dear Diary,

Okay, I admit it. I'm nervous about the cook-off today. I didn't expect to have to *compete* to be the Porter House chef. Especially against my new friend, Brigitte!

I bet Brigitte's a great cook just like her famous mother.

Mary-Kate isn't worried. She gave me a pep talk at breakfast. "Believe me, Ashley," Mary-Kate said. "You're the best cook in the First Form. Mom's recipe won that Chicago cooking contest because all the judges loved her potpie, right?"

"Yep." I nodded.

"And you've got the exact same recipe, right?" Mary-Kate sipped her orange juice and stared at me.

"I've got the recipe she kept in her recipe box," I said. It's one of my most cherished possessions.

"Then *your* Chunky Chicken Under Cover will be the same as *Mom's* Chunky Chicken Under Cover. A prizewinner! All you have to do is follow directions, and you'll win the cook-off."

"I hope you're right," I said.

"I wonder if Brigitte is nervous," Mary-Kate said.

I looked over my shoulder. Brigitte was sitting at the next table by herself. *Why doesn't she come over? Does Brigitte think I'll be mad if she wins?* I wondered. I'd be disappointed, but I wouldn't be angry. It was a contest, and the best recipe would win.

"She looks like she could use some company," Mary-Kate said.

"Exactly what I was thinking!" I grinned and picked up my tray. "Let's go."

Brigitte looked up as we put our trays down on her table.

"Hi. Is it okay if we join you?" I asked, to be polite.

"Uh, yes." Brigitte put her napkin on her plate. She had only eaten half her eggs and toast. "But I have to go."

"Oh, that's too bad," I said. "Mary-Kate wants to get to know you better."

"I can't right now." Brigitte stood up and left.

Mary-Kate frowned. "Did I do something wrong?"

I shook my head. "I bet Brigitte just wants to get ready for the cook-off tonight. I know I've got a lot to do."

And I didn't have time to waste. I ran back to my room as soon as I finished eating. At least it was Saturday, and we didn't have classes.

First I had to check the ingredients in the recipe. We had permission to use the dorm kitchen for the cook-off. Miss Viola probably had some of the basic things I needed. I'd have to get the rest at the store.

I keep Mom's recipe in a small box with my other special treasures. It's made of wood, with a silver design on the lid. My dad gave it to me for Christmas when I was six. I've got hair from my first haircut, the first tooth I lost, and my mother's picture. I keep the box in the back of my desk drawer.

I felt kind of warm inside when I put the box on my desk. I miss my mom, and my keepsakes make me feel closer to her. My eyes got a little teary when I pulled out the winning recipe. The paper was folded in half and so old, it was a little yellow.

An awful thought suddenly hit me. *What if something happens to it?*

Phoebe came into the room then. "What are you doing, Ashley?" she asked.

"Just getting out my recipe," I said. "I'm going to copy it and save it on my computer so nothing happens to the one my mother wrote."

"Good thinking." Phoebe perched on the edge of her bed. "I'm going to make the menus."

"That's great," I said, unfolding the handwritten recipe.

I love to cook, Diary, just like my mom. She made up her own recipes and tested them on us. She wanted to put the best ones in a cookbook, but then she died. Maybe someday I'll be a great chef, and then I can write that cookbook for her.

I looked over my mom's recipe for Chunky Chicken Under Cover one more time. The recipe was so old, some of the writing was faded.

The top half was a list of all the ingredients. The directions were written on the bottom half. I looked for the star my mother always placed next to a special ingredient or a special cooking hint.

"There's no star!" I gasped. "I just know my mom put one here!"

"It's got to be there." Phoebe came over to look.

I held the paper under the light.

"Is that it?" Phoebe pointed to the crease where the paper was folded.

I could just barely make out the star.

But the writing next to the star was completely worn.

I know the secret ingredient is what makes Chunky Chicken Under Cover so great, Diary.

Yet I don't have a clue what the secret ingredient is!

Dear Diary,

Since I'm the head waitress, I held the first waitstaff meeting today. Campbell, Lexy Martin, Cheryl, and Layne Wagner all want to be waitresses for our restaurant. They think taking food to the tables will be more fun than making it.

There's just one problem, Diary. Carrying food is the *only* thing we know about being a waitress!

"Are we going to use trays?" Lexy asked.

"What if the plates fall?" Layne looked worried.

"Maybe there's a trick to carrying full trays," Campbell said.

"Without spilling anything," Lexy added.

"What if I forget which order goes to which customer?" Cheryl frowned. "There must be a trick to that, too."

"But how do we find out?" Campbell asked. "I don't think the library has a book about this."

"You're the head waitress, Mary-Kate," Cheryl said. "Got any brilliant ideas?"

"Actually, I do!" I knew the perfect way to find out everything waitresses do.

After the meeting I left the dorm to walk into town. We're allowed to leave the White Oak campus on weekends. I had a plan. The best way to learn how to wait tables was to ask a real waitress.

The Burger Bistro is my favorite place in town to go for hamburgers. I got to the restaurant just after one in the afternoon. A lot of shoppers were still eating lunch.

I sat at a table near the kitchen. My plan was to order, eat, and ask questions. I had a notebook with me so I could write everything down.

A waitress came over to my table and handed me a menu. "Would you like something to drink?" she asked. Her name tag said RHONDA. She was wearing black pants, a white shirt, and a green apron. She had short blonde hair.

"A cherry soda, please," I said. "Do you always take the drink order first?"

"Unless people are in a hurry." Rhonda looked at me quizzically. "Are you ready to order your food?"

I ordered the same thing I always did at Burger Bistro. "A cheeseburger and fries," I said.

Rhonda wrote both items on an order pad. Then she went straight to the kitchen. She wasn't carrying anything when she came back out a moment later.

I looked over my notes to make sure I had written everything down.

Then Rhonda was back with my soda.

"Where did this come from?" I asked, surprised. Rhonda didn't have a soda when she left the kitchen a minute ago.

"You ordered a soda, right?" Rhonda looked worried she had made a mistake.

"Yes, I did." I nodded. "I meant, where did you get it? From the kitchen?"

"From the machine in the wait station." Rhonda pointed to a walled-off area across the room. "It's where we keep glasses, ketchup, coffeepots, the soda machine – all the extra stuff customers need."

I wrote that down, too.

"Why are you taking notes?" Rhonda asked. "Are you writing a report for school?"

"Not exactly," I said. "Our dorm has to run a restaurant for a school project. I have so many questions about waiting on tables. I could really use some help."

"I'd love to help you," Rhonda said, "but I'm too busy right now."

"That's okay." I was disappointed, but I tried not to show it. "I can learn a lot just by watching."

That's what I did, Diary. I ate my cheeseburger very slowly and studied everything Rhonda did. I was amazed at how much waitresses have to do!

Rhonda took orders, delivered drinks and food, picked up dirty dishes, cleaned tables, got ketchup and other things people needed, wrote up checks, and collected money. She worked faster than I could write!

Almost all the customers were gone when I swallowed my last fry.

"Do you need to leave now?" Rhonda asked when she came back to get my plate.

"No." I shook my head. "Do you have time to answer some questions?"

"I can do better than that," Rhonda said. "My manager said I can give you some real behind-the-scenes experience."

"You can?" I couldn't believe it!

"He said it's okay because it's for school," Rhonda explained. "Are you ready to work?"

Boy, was I ready! We walked over to the wait station and I stashed my notebook and bag in a cupboard.

"First we're going to marry the ketchup and mustard," Rhonda said.

"Are they in love?" I joked.

"Not with each other," Rhonda laughed. She gathered the mustard and ketchup bottles that were almost empty. Then she showed me what to do.

I put one ketchup bottle over another with the openings together. That way the ketchup in the top bottle would fall into the bottom bottle—and the almost empty bottle would get full. I carefully balanced the top bottle. Then I let go.

The top bottle wobbled. Then it fell with a loud clattering sound. Everyone in the Bistro turned to look.

"Oops!" I cringed.

Ketchup was splattered all over the table. There were red spots on everything—including me!

Rhonda just laughed. "I'll clean this up. Can you clear the dishes from that table over there?"

I looked where Rhonda pointed. Two elderly ladies were sitting at a table by the window. They were drinking coffee. Their salad plates were pushed aside.

"No problem," I said. I wanted to show Rhonda that I could take care of the customers.

The two ladies were talking. They didn't seem to notice me when I walked up to the table. I didn't want to be rude so I didn't interrupt. I just picked up their salad plates.

"Wait!" one lady said. "I'm not finished with that."

There were two bites of salad left on the plate.

"I'm sorry," I said. I should have asked first.

The lady reached for the plate as I started to put it back on the table. We both let go at the same time. The plate fell and bounced off the table. Lettuce spilled on the carpet!

"Well, I don't want it *now*," the lady said.

"I, uh – " I stammered.

What do waitresses do when this happens? I wondered. I didn't see Rhonda anywhere. So I started picking up the lettuce.

Rhonda came over. "Is there a problem?"

"I wasn't finished with my salad," the lady said.

"Would you like another one?" Rhonda asked.

"No, thank you," the lady said. Then she started talking to her friend.

Rhonda smiled at me. "Why don't you do something safe – like fill the saltshakers?"

That sounded good to me. I filled every saltshaker there. Then I waited for Rhonda by the wait station when I was done. So far, being a waitress wasn't as exciting as I had imagined. In fact, this part was boring. I wanted to do the good stuff – like take orders.

"Could you take these into the kitchen for me?" a waitress named Gail said, handing me four glasses. "Just put them in the rack by the dishwasher."

"Uh – okay." I gripped two glasses in each hand as I walked toward the swinging double doors into the kitchen.

I started to go in the door on the left just as another waitress named Lydia was leaving the kitchen. Lydia was holding a tray full of dishes. She stopped suddenly so she wouldn't crash into me.

I backed up a step. That's when I noticed the signs on the doors. Oh, no! I was going *in* the OUT door.

Lydia gasped. Her tray was tilted, and all the plates on it were sliding off!

Chapter 3

Saturday

Dear Diary,

I thought the dishes would crash on the floor. And I was sure the manager would kick me out. But I was lucky.

Lydia balanced the tray and luckily none of the plates fell off!

"I am *so* sorry," I said.

"Don't worry about it," Lydia said.

Now I know why there are *two* kitchen doors, Diary. All the waitresses go IN the door on the right. They come OUT the door on the left. That way they don't bump into one another.

Then I remembered I was still holding four glasses. I went into the kitchen through the IN door.

The kitchen was big and busy. The dishwashing area was on the right. I put the glasses in a special rack for glasses.

The cook, whose name was Henry, was standing between the stoves and a long metal counter. Warming lights hung over the counter. Plates of hot food sat on the counter under the lights.

Rhonda came into the kitchen and put some dirty plates in a tub. "I hear you broke the number one rule around here," she said. "Never go in the 'out' door." She picked up an empty tray. Then she grinned at me. "Everybody goes in or out the wrong door at least once. It's no biggie."

What a relief. I'll *never* make that mistake again!

Rhonda explained how food ordering worked. She tore off the top page from her order pad. "We call this a ticket, and we hang it on this wheel," she said. She clipped the ticket to the round rack on the counter. "Always put it to the left of the last ticket."

"Why?" I asked.

"So the cook can make the meals in the order the tickets arrive," Rhonda said. She checked the ticket by the plates under the warmers. "This is mine."

Rhonda put the plates on her tray and the ticket on the spindle. "That's so Henry doesn't make the same order again."

I followed Rhonda out the OUT door.

The restaurant was almost full again. Four more people were waiting to sit down. This was my big chance!

"It's so busy. I could take a table, Rhonda," I said.

"Thanks, Mary-Kate, but we can handle it." Rhonda left to seat the four new people.

Eight more people came in. Gail and Lydia each took a table of two. Four people were still waiting by the door. Then Rhonda came to the wait station for drinks.

"If you need help, I can wait on those new people," I offered.

Rhonda hesitated. Then she shook her head. "No, I'd better get them."

I was so frustrated, Diary! I was sure I could handle one table if Rhonda would just give me a chance.

I stood by the wait station in case someone needed help. I filled pitchers with iced tea and water for free refills, and I married more ketchup bottles.

"Mary-Kate!" Rhonda said, rushing over. "Can you take the table of three in the corner?"

"Do you mean seat them?" I asked.

Rhonda shook her head. "No, I mean *wait* on the table."

"Sure!" I took the menus and the order pad that Rhonda gave me. "No problem."

Finally! Rhonda was letting me wait on customers. By myself! I went to the table, hoping I'd remember everything.

Then I stopped, shocked.

My cousin Jeremy Burke was sitting at the table with two of his friends from Harrington Academy, Carter Black and Trevor Apfelbaum. At least my first real customers weren't strangers. "Hi, Jeremy,"

I said. I handed a menu to each of the boys.

"You work here, Mary-Kate?" Jeremy asked. "For real?"

Jeremy loves to play pranks on people. He especially likes to play pranks on Ashley and me. *Maybe he thinks I'm playing a joke on him,* I thought.

"I'm helping out today," I explained.

"This should be good," Trevor said.

Trevor can be very annoying, Diary. He teased me the whole time we had fencing class together.

"I've never had a real job," Carter said. "I think it's cool, Mary-Kate."

"Thanks," I said. Carter is totally nice and cute. I grinned and asked for their drink order.

"Do we get free refills with sodas?" Trevor asked.

"We only have free refills with water or iced tea," I explained.

"Iced tea," Jeremy said. "I'm really thirsty and I'll want lots of refills."

"Me, too," Trevor said. "Iced tea. Why don't you have free refills with soda?"

"I don't know," I said. "Maybe soda costs a lot more than iced tea."

Carter wanted iced tea, too. I went back to the wait station and filled three glasses with iced tea.

"Thanks," Carter said when I set his glass down.

"Where's my slice of lemon?" Jeremy asked.

"I need a straw," Trevor said. "And a spoon with a long handle."

Oops! I had forgotten the extras.

"Oh, uh – I'll get them!" I turned to go.

Jeremy called me back. "Bring some extra sugar, okay?"

I looked at the container of sugar. "It's full."

Trevor took out five packets. Carter took three.

Jeremy took the rest of the packets. "It's empty now." He ripped off the tops and poured the sugar into his iced tea.

I hurried back to the wait station. I put lemons and sugar packets in dishes. Then I carried both dishes back to the table with straws and spoons.

"Are you ready to order?" I took out my pen and pad.

"Hamburger and fries," Trevor said.

"Wait a minute!" Jeremy said.

"What?" I stopped writing.

Jeremy leaned across the table and whispered to Trevor. Trevor nodded and sat back. "Make that a cheeseburger instead," Trevor said.

"Okay." I crossed out "ham" and wrote "cheese" above it. "Who's next?" I asked, but Trevor wasn't done.

"And onion rings instead of fries," Trevor finished.

"Are you sure?" I asked first. When Trevor nodded, I crossed out "fries" and wrote "rings." Then I looked at Jeremy. "Have you decided?"

"I'll have a cheeseburger and fries," Jeremy said.

I hesitated before I wrote anything. I never forget that Jeremy likes to play tricks. "Are you sure?"

"Yep." Jeremy nodded. "I'm sure."

I smiled and wrote down his order.

"Wait," Jeremy said. "I'll have onion rings, too."

My smile froze. I knew Trevor and Jeremy were deliberately giving me a hard time. But I didn't know what to do about it. The customer is always right. Then I had a brainstorm. "Sorry, Jeremy," I said. "We're out of onion rings."

"But – " Jeremy blinked. "Trevor ordered onion rings."

"He got the last order," I said. It was hard to keep a straight face. The restaurant had plenty of onion rings. I just wanted to give Jeremy a taste of his own medicine.

"That's too bad," Carter said. "I wanted onion rings with my hamburger."

"Let me check with the kitchen again," I said. "If we have three orders of onion rings left, you guys can have them."

"Thanks, Mary-Kate!" Jeremy looked relieved.

I changed Jeremy's "fries" to "rings" and wrote down Carter's order. I took the ticket to the kitchen, but the wheel was too high. I couldn't reach it!

"Need some help hanging that?" Henry, the cook, asked.

I handed him the ticket. "Sorry I had to cross out stuff. Can you read it?"

Henry read the order back to me. "Two cheeseburgers, both with rings, and a hamburger with rings."

"That's it!" I felt better when I got back to the wait station. I took ketchup and mustard to Jeremy's table.

"We could collect aluminum cans," Carter said.

"The town pays people to pick up litter," Trevor said.

"Getting money for cans isn't really a community service project," Jeremy pointed out.

"Is Harrington doing community service for holiday projects?" I asked.

Jeremy nodded. "But we can't think of anything."

"What holiday projects are you doing at White Oak?" Carter asked.

"All the First Form dorms will be holiday restaurants next Saturday night," I said.

"Cool!" Carter grinned.

"It'll be fun," I said. "But we need at least twenty reservations. So spread the word. Have everyone come to Porter House."

The boys wanted more iced tea and more sugar. I hurried back to the wait station and grabbed the pitcher and sugar. Then I rushed back to the table.

"We could take old people shopping," Carter suggested.

"No, we can't," Jeremy said. "We don't drive."

Trevor made a face. "I hate shopping."

"Here you go, guys." I smiled and poured more iced tea into Trevor's glass.

"That's not iced tea," Trevor said. "It's water."

"It is?" I peered into the pitcher. It *was* water! "Sorry. I'll be right back."

I went back to the wait station again. I got Trevor a new glass and checked to make sure I had the iced-tea pitcher. Being a waitress isn't easy, Diary!

"Your order's ready, Mary-Kate," Lydia said.

"Already?" I decided to take the iced tea first. Then I went into the kitchen to get my order.

And that's when I realized I was too small to carry a big tray. I had to take three plates, but I only had two hands! I decided to make two trips.

I checked my ticket and the plates. There were

two cheeseburgers with onion rings, and one hamburger with rings. I put my ticket on the spindle. Then I took the two cheeseburgers to Jeremy's table.

"I know!" Carter snapped his fingers. "We could walk around singing songs, like in the movies!"

"My voice cracks when I sing," Jeremy said.

"I sound like a frog," Trevor said.

I almost laughed as I put the plates on the table.

"Then our community service project could be to *stop* singing!" Carter said and grinned.

I rushed back to the kitchen. I grabbed the hamburger and onion rings and brought the plate to the table. "Will there be anything else?" I asked.

"No, this is great," Jeremy said. "Thanks for getting us the last three orders of onion rings."

"You're welcome," I said.

The rest of my one-table shift went great. Jeremy and his friends couldn't agree on a community service project, but they were happy with the burgers. They left me a two-dollar tip!

I cleared the table and put down new place mats and silverware. Then I went to thank Henry for his help. Rhonda came into the kitchen before I left.

"Maybe Mary-Kate can work that dinner," Henry said.

"I was just about to ask her," Rhonda said.

"Ask me what?" I looked from Henry to Rhonda.

"A lot of police officers and firefighters have to work on the holiday," Rhonda said. "The Burger Bistro is having a holiday family dinner for them and their families *before* Christmas."

"Turkey with all the fixings," Henry said. He winked. "And Santa Claus will be here to give presents to the kids."

"And I could use another good waitress," Rhonda said. "If you want to volunteer."

"I'd love to," I said. "But I made a lot of mistakes today."

"And you handled every single one." Rhonda smiled. "I'm in charge, and I want you."

"I'll do everything I can to help," I said. "You've got yourself a waitress."

"Order up, Rhonda," Henry said.

Rhonda had to deliver the food while it was still hot. "I'll call you with the details, Mary-Kate."

"Great!" I gave Rhonda my number at Porter House. As I left I waved and said good-bye to Henry. I was totally thrilled that Rhonda wanted me to work for her. Waiting on tables at the Porter House restaurant would be easy after this!

Dear Diary,

I've tried everything, and I can't figure out the secret ingredient in Mom's potpie recipe.

Phoebe stayed to help this morning. When we held the recipe under my desk lamp, we found the star. But we still couldn't read the writing after it.

"Face it, Ashley," Phoebe finally said. "The handwriting is too faded to read."

I didn't want to admit that. But Phoebe was right, Diary. The writing was completely gone.

"Why don't you go ice skating with me?" Phoebe pulled out mittens and a hat from her dresser.

"No, thanks," I said.

"Fresh air and hot chocolate might make you feel better," she said.

Nothing would make me feel better. Except finding the secret ingredient. I didn't tell Phoebe that.

"I have to try to find the secret ingredient," I said. "I really want Porter House to win."

"And a pizza party," Phoebe said.

After Phoebe left, I called my father. He's a professor who does research all over the world. Right now he was in the Amazon. That's why

Mary-Kate and I go to boarding school. "Hi, Dad! It's Ashley."

"What a surprise!" Dad exclaimed. "What's going on?"

"I'm making Mom's Chunky Chicken Under Cover recipe in a cooking contest," I said.

"That's great, Ashley," he said.

"Except the secret ingredient rubbed off of the recipe," I explained. "Do you know what it is?"

"No, I don't. I'm sorry, sweetheart." My father sighed."

Before I hung up, Dad and I talked about his work. He misses us as much as we miss him.

Who else might know the secret ingredient?

I could only think of one other person. Great-Aunt Morgan was my mom's favorite aunt. I called her. "Hi, Aunt Morgan! This is Ashley."

"I'm so glad to hear from you," Great-aunt Morgan said.

I got right to the point. "Do you have my mom's prizewinning recipe for Chunky Chicken Under Cover?"

"No, Ashley, I don't." Aunt Morgan sounded sad. "I wish I did. I've never tasted a better chicken potpie."

"Did she tell you the secret ingredient?" I asked.

"No," Great-aunt Morgan said. "She didn't tell anyone. It was top secret."

I felt totally depressed when I hung up. I sat staring out the window, remembering.

I used to watch my mother roll the dough and mix the sauce, Diary. She was always very careful putting on the top crust so the dough wouldn't tear. Then I suddenly remembered that she had told *me* the secret ingredient!

But that happened a long time ago, Diary. I don't remember what she said!

And without the secret ingredient, Chunky Chicken Under Cover will just be plain old ordinary chicken pot yuck!

Chapter 4

Saturday Night

Dear Diary,

Phoebe came back early from ice skating. She wanted to help me make my chicken potpie. I was glad for the company.

Phoebe and I went to the dorm kitchen at five o'clock to make the cook-off potpie. At seven everyone would meet in the lounge to vote on what Brigitte and I had cooked.

Miss Viola had all my ingredients. The chicken, the vegetables, and the pastry squares were in the refrigerator. Everything else was on the counter.

"Where's Brigitte?" Phoebe asked.

"She asked to use the kitchen earlier," Miss Viola said.

I nodded. Desserts could be made ahead of time. Brigitte had probably wanted to cook alone so nobody would learn her recipe secrets.

"She did a great job of cleaning up." Miss Viola said, looking around. "The kitchen is spotless.

"I'll be over here if you need me," she said. She sat in a chair in the corner and opened a magazine.

"So where do we start?" Phoebe asked me.

"First we cook the chicken and chop the veggies," I said.

I put the boneless chicken meat into boiling water. Phoebe sliced mushrooms and carrots. I chopped the garlic and onion. Onions really do make you cry, Diary!

"Cold water will help," Phoebe said. She dabbed my eyes with a wet cloth.

"Thanks, Phoebe," I said. "That feels a little better." I blinked back another tear.

"Just don't cry in the pie, Ashley," Phoebe warned me. "Nobody will vote for a chef who makes a salty, soggy crust!"

It was weird to be laughing and crying at the same time. We cut chicken and potatoes into cubes.

"Now the filling," I said.

I got a large saucepan from the cabinet. Phoebe handed me the ingredients.

All the ingredients but the secret one, I thought.

I melted butter. Then I added the onions, garlic, and flour. The mixture cooked for two minutes. Next I put in chicken broth, salt and pepper, the chicken, and vegetables. I set the filling aside, turned the oven on, and got the pastry squares from the refrigerator.

"Can we both roll out the dough?" Phoebe asked.

"Flatten away." I handed Phoebe a rolling pin and a pastry square. We each rolled out dough for the crust. I put one of the crusts in a deep, square baking dish. Then I poured in the filling.

"Do we put the top on now?" Phoebe asked.

I hesitated. I knew I was forgetting a step. I checked the recipe. We had done every step in the directions. The "cover" was the last thing before baking. *Maybe we don't really need the secret ingredient,* I told myself. *It's probably no big deal.*

Phoebe carefully placed the rolled pastry over the top of the dish. I trimmed the extra dough off the sides. Then I pinched the edge of the crusts together. I made four cuts in the top to let the steam out. And we were done!

Phoebe grinned. "It looks fantastic!"

I put the potpie in the oven.

Phoebe and I did homework while we waited for the potpie to bake. The top crust was golden brown when I took it out of the oven an hour later.

Phoebe inhaled. "This smells so good."

"Let's hope it tastes good, too!"

I put the hot dish on a tray with a large spoon. Phoebe carried plastic forks and paper plates. Everyone was in the lounge when we got there.

Except Brigitte.

Where is she? I wondered.

Phoebe passed out plates and forks for samples.

"It looks just like Mom's Chunky Chicken Under Cover," Mary-Kate said. "I knew you could do it!"

"It does look the same, doesn't it?" I said, proud of myself.

Then Brigitte came into the lounge with a tray of éclairs.

The flaky pastry shells were filled with a fluffy vanilla custard. The pastry was topped with a chocolate glaze, whipped cream, and cherries.

If those éclairs taste as good as they look, I'm not going to win the cook-off, I thought. My mouth started to water, Diary!

"Wow!" Kristen exclaimed. "Those look great!"

"Thank you," Brigitte said softly. She cut each éclair into several pieces and put the pieces on paper plates.

All the girls crowded around Brigitte.

Only Mary-Kate, Campbell, and Phoebe tried my chicken potpie first.

"This éclair is the best dessert ever!" Brooke said.

"Heavenly!" Cheryl gushed.

"It tastes fantastic, Brigitte!" Elise said, swallowing her little piece of éclair. "Are there more?"

"Sorry. Not tonight," Brigitte said.

"Have a taste of Ashley's Chunky Chicken Under Cover, Elise," Phoebe said. "There are *two* people in the cook-off."

"Right!" Elise took a sample and a fork. She chewed thoughtfully. "Not bad, Ashley."

Campbell nodded. "I think your chicken stuff tastes good."

Mary-Kate swallowed, then smiled. "This is great, Ashley."

"Thanks." I took a bite of my potpie. That's when I knew Mary-Kate was just being nice. The potpie was bland without the secret ingredient.

"Do you want to taste Brigitte's dessert, Ashley?" Phoebe asked, handing me a sample.

The instant my taste buds met Brigitte's éclair I knew I had lost the cook-off. The chocolate glaze and custard were smooth and sweet.

Everyone raised their hands for Brigitte's éclair when Summer called for the vote. Even me, Diary! Fair's fair. Brigitte's dessert *was* better than Chunky Chicken Under Cover without the secret ingredient.

"Super!" Summer said and grinned. "We all agreed. Porter House will have an all-dessert restaurant!"

Everyone cheered. I was disappointed, but I wasn't too upset. Being the chef might help Brigitte make more friends.

"Those éclairs were amazing, Brigitte," I said. "You really deserve to be the Porter House chef. Congratulations!"

"Thanks, Ashley," Brigitte mumbled. "I have to go. I have to call my mother."

"Sure," I said. "She'll be thrilled you won the – "

Brigitte turned and walked away.

I don't think I said anything to upset her, Diary. But I can't figure out why Brigitte is always rushing off. Maybe she doesn't want to make friends. Maybe she just likes to be alone.

Sunday

Dear Diary,

I didn't vote for Ashley's potpie. I still feel guilty, Diary, even though Ashley forgave me at breakfast.

"Are you really disappointed?" I asked my sister.

"*I* am," Phoebe answered. "Ashley should have won the cook-off."

"But Brigitte's dessert was the best," Ashley said. "Even I voted for her!"

"So you're not mad at me?" I wanted to be sure.

"No!" Ashley laughed. "I want Porter House to win Jerome Dupont's five-star rating."

I relaxed. Ashley is a good sport.

"I have to go," Lexy said. "I have a geometry test tomorrow. Mary-Kate, are you coming to study?"

I have to take the same test, Diary. Lexy and I left Ashley and Phoebe and went to the library to study. As soon as we sat down, Dana came over to our table.

"What are you two doing?" Dana asked.

"Geometry," Lexy answered. "What about you?"

"I'm researching Jerome Dupont," Dana said.

Lexy blinked. "Why?"

"Because it's going to get us five stars," Dana said. Dana always assumes she'll win.

"Mr. Dupont might not pick Phipps House, Dana," I said.

"He will definitely choose Phipps House." Dana sounded absolutely certain.

"How come you're so sure?" Lexy asked.

"We're serving Rock Cornish game hen stuffed with wild rice," Dana explained. "It's Mr. Dupont's favorite meal."

Lexy frowned. "How do you know?"

Dana smiled. "I read some of Mr. Dupont's old columns to find out."

That figures, I thought. Research wasn't cheating. It just proved how much Dana wanted to win.

"There's no way Porter House can beat us," Dana added.

"I wouldn't bet on that," I said.

"I would." Dana smiled. "What should we bet?"

I wasn't expecting Dana to actually bet, Diary. But I couldn't back down.

"The loser makes the winner's bed for a week," I said, and we shook hands.

"What if Mr. Dupont picks Marble Manor?" Lexy asked. Marble Manor is the other First Form dorm.

"Then the bet is off," Dana said. "But you'd better practise making beds, Mary-Kate, because you don't have a chance. Kristen told me Porter House voted to have an all-dessert restaurant."

Sometimes it's no fun having Dana's best friend in my dorm, Diary.

"So?" Lexy asked.

"So that's not a real restaurant, is it? I mean, I've never been to a restaurant that just serves dessert." Dana turned and strutted out the library door.

Lexy looked stunned. "What if Dana is right, Mary-Kate? What if having nothing but desserts is a mistake?"

I was wondering the same thing.

"Let's find out what the other dorm is doing," I

said. "If making only dessert *is* a mistake, we should know now."

Lexy and I studied for two hours. Then we headed straight to Marble Manor. We had to check out their menu.

Amber Fleming answered the door at Marble Manor. Amber told us that Natalie Pittman was their chef.

Natalie is a great cook. Last year she made an awesome pizza for her roommate's birthday. Brandy Oliver, Ellen Withers, and Blair Clark were on Natalie's kitchen committee. They were all having a meeting in the lounge.

"Mary-Kate is here. She has a question," Amber said.

"About what?" Natalie asked.

"What kind of restaurant you're having," Lexy said.

"We're doing a traditional English dinner," Brandy said. "Roast beef and Yorkshire pudding."

"We're cooking string beans too," Ellen added. "And a chocolate cake for dessert."

"Sounds fabulous," I said. "Good luck with it."

Lexy and I felt pretty low as we walked back to Porter House. The other First Form dorms were all making fancy, full-course dinners.

How can an all-dessert restaurant compete with that, Diary? We can't!

And if Phipps House wins, I'll be making Dana's bed all next week! I can't let that happen.

Chapter 5

Sunday

Dear Diary,

Lexy and I called an emergency meeting as soon as we got back to the dorm.

"What's going on?" Ashley sat beside me.

"You'll see," I said.

Elise and Brooke waved Brigitte over when she came in. It looked as if she was finally making friends.

"Everyone's here except Phoebe," Lexy said.

"Phoebe's at the computer centre," Ashley explained. "But I'll tell her what she missed."

"Lexy and I did some investigating," I began. "We found out that *all* the other First Form restaurants are making fancy dinners: main course, vegetables, dessert – the whole works. We think Porter House should serve a full meal, too."

"Or we won't have a chance of winning the five-star rating," Lexy added.

"What would we make?" Summer asked.

"Chunky Chicken Under Cover!" Phoebe stood in the doorway and waved a paper. "Ashley's recipe really is a blue-ribbon winner. I found an article about it on the Internet."

"Really?" Ashley looked up with surprise.

"Take a look." Phoebe gave the printout of the article to Cheryl to pass to Ashley. "It's all about how your mom won that cooking contest in Chicago!"

"Well, that's good enough for me," Jolene said. "Let's make Ashley's potpie, too."

"But Ashley's potpie was just okay," Brooke pointed out. "I mean, it was kind of blah."

I rose to my sister's defence. "Ashley has our mother's *exact* recipe. I'm sure she can perfect it by Saturday."

"This article raves about Ashley's mom's chicken potpie," Cheryl said.

Ashley took the paper from Cheryl.

"I nominate Ashley to cook the main course," Cheryl said.

Phoebe quickly jumped in. "I second that!"

"All in favor?" I asked. The vote was unanimous. But the meeting wasn't over. "What else should we have?"

"I make a great green salad," Phoebe said.

"With some rolls," Campbell said. "Then we'll top the whole thing off with one of Brigitte's fantastic desserts."

"What kind of dessert will you make, Brigitte?" Summer asked.

I hadn't stopped to think how Brigitte would take the change. I hoped she wasn't too upset. After all, there was no rule against having *two* chefs.

"Oh, uh – " Brigitte stammered. "I have so many recipes, it's hard to choose."

I glanced over at her. She looked totally uncomfortable. *It must be because she's shy,* I thought. "You don't have to decide right now, Brigitte," I said.

"Whatever you choose will be great," Elise said and grinned. "That five-star rating is almost ours!"

"Fame and pizza!" Cheryl cheered. "Woohoo!"

That's when I realised Ashley hadn't said a word. I thought she'd be thrilled everyone wanted her to cook.

But Ashley wasn't smiling, Diary. She was staring at the article about Mom's cooking contest. I wanted to ask what was wrong. But there was more restaurant business to discuss.

"Everybody has to make a supply list," Lexy said. "Food, decorations, whatever we need. Then someone has to add up the cost and place the orders."

"Don't pick me," Summer said. "I love to shop. But I never keep track of what I spend. I'd go way over budget."

Everyone laughed. Then they all turned to stare at me.

I blinked. "Does the head waitress usually do the ordering?"

"You get good grades in math, Mary-Kate," Campbell said. "You'll make sure we don't spend more than the budget."

The phone in the hall rang. Phoebe went to answer it.

"Who wants Mary-Kate to do the ordering?" Lexy asked.

All the hands went up. I had another job.

Phoebe came back from answering the phone. "Someone named Rhonda left a message for you, Mary-Kate. You have a volunteers' meeting at the Burger Bistro tomorrow night."

"Volunteer for what, Mary-Kate?" Kristen asked.

"Helping serve dinner to police officers and firefighters who have to work on the holiday," I said. "The Burger Bistro is giving them a dinner *before* Christmas so they can eat with their families."

"Isn't that a lot to do?" Campbell asked.

"It's for a good cause," I said.

"I meant doing *two* jobs for Porter House *and* volunteering for the Burger Bistro *and* schoolwork," Campbell said.

"It does seem like a lot, Mary-Kate," Summer agreed.

"But helping people is what we're supposed to do this time of year," I said. "Don't worry. I can handle it."

Dear Diary,

Guess what happened. Everyone at Porter House wants me to make Chunky Chicken Under Cover after all. So now, Diary, Brigitte and I are co-chefs.

I wish I could be happier. Everyone is counting on me to help win the five-star rating. But I still don't know the secret ingredient.

Brigitte isn't happy, either, Diary. I don't know why. I tried to talk to her after the emergency meeting.

"Working together will make this project even more fun, Brigitte," I said. "And a lot less work."

Brigitte just nodded. She looked distracted. Or worried.

"This way you only have to make *one* dessert," I said. "Not a whole bunch. Do you need help trying to pick one?"

"No," Brigitte snapped. "I can do it."

"I didn't mean – " There was no point trying to explain. Brigitte walked out.

What's her problem, Diary? I know Brigitte is

shy, but she's not usually rude. I thought we were friends. Friends are happy for each other. And they help each other out.

But Brigitte doesn't want my help.

And she isn't happy that we're both chefs.

Maybe Brigitte doesn't want to share the credit with me if Porter House wins the five-star rating. That's hard to believe. But nothing else makes sense. The whole dorm should share the credit. Brigitte has been acting really weird ever since we decided to have a cook-off.

But Brigitte isn't my only problem. I *still* have to figure out the secret ingredient. I thought I might recognize the secret ingredient if I saw it. Mrs. Bromsky, the dining hall lady, said I could look at her herbs and spices after dinner Sunday night.

Brigitte was standing by the big stove when I walked into the dining hall kitchen.

"Hi, Brigitte!" I was glad to see her. I wanted to fix things between us. "I didn't expect to find you here."

"Mrs. Bromsky gave me permission to cook," Brigitte said. She stirred something in a pot on the stove. "She'll be back in a few minutes."

"Mrs. Bromsky gave me permission to check the spices," I said. "What are you making?"

Brigitte moved so I couldn't look into the pot. "It's just an experiment."

She's probably guarding a secret recipe, I thought. Recipes are a chef's most prized possessions. If Brigitte didn't want to discuss her recipe, that was okay with me.

"Maybe you can help me," I said.

"Help with what?" Brigitte asked.

"One of the seasonings in my mom's recipe is too faded to read," I explained. "Everything about the potpie I baked for the cook-off was the same as my mom's. Except for the taste."

"Wasn't the recipe in the article that Phoebe found?" Brigitte said, taking her spoon out of the pot. She turned to look at me.

"No, it wasn't." I sighed.

Phoebe had found the article because she was looking for my mom's recipe. She knew I needed the secret ingredient. But the contest recipes had been published on a different page. That page wasn't in the online newspaper archives.

"Did you taste my potpie, Brigitte?" I asked.

I moved to the racks of spices. I read the labels on the jars to myself. *Allspice, basil, bay leaves . . .*

"Yes," Brigitte said. "It was very . . . American."

"The missing seasoning gives it a zesty tang," I

said. "Do you know what spice it might be?"

I read more labels to myself. *Celery salt, chives, cinnamon, cloves . . .*

"Different blends of herbs and spices create different aromas and flavors," Brigitte said. "But there are a zillion possible combinations. So I can't possibly guess."

I nodded. "I see your point. Thanks, anyway."

But I couldn't give up.

I kept reading. *Dill, garlic salt, ginger . . .*

"Oh, no!" Brigitte shrieked and jumped back from the stove.

"What's the matter?" I sprang to help her.

"See what you made me do!" Brigitte yelled.

I looked at the pot on the stove. Brigitte's mysterious mixture was boiling over. Dark brown goo bubbled inside the pot. Globs dribbled down the sides. "Me?" I was stunned.

"I stopped stirring to talk to you," Brigitte said.

I didn't want to say anything, Diary, but I think Brigitte's recipe was ruined *before* it boiled over.

And Brigitte saw me wrinkle my nose.

"Are you making fun of me, Ashley?" Brigitte's eyes flashed. She was furious.

"No, Brigitte!" I couldn't let her think that! "Honest."

"Now I have to clean up this mess." Brigitte turned the stove off.

"I'm really sorry," I said. "Let me help you – "

"Forget it." Brigitte moved the pan to a cold burner. "I just want to be left alone."

I didn't want to make things worse. I left, but I was upset, too.

Brigitte and I were becoming good friends before the cook-off. Now it looks like our friendship is over because of a silly contest.

Chapter 6

Monday

Dear Diary,

Good news! The geometry test was easy. I'm sure I got an *A*. What a relief!

MARY-KATE'S DIARY

But I had lots of other work today. I had to go to another meeting at the Burger Bistro for Rhonda's volunteers. But first I had a Porter House restaurant meeting.

Campbell and I sat on the sofa in the Porter House lounge. Summer came running in, very excited. "We've already got twenty reservations!" Summer held up a notebook with the names written in a neat column.

Twenty was the minimum number of reservations Mrs. Pritchard said we needed in order to participate.

"That's terrific, Summer!" I said, giving her a thumbs-up.

"And we've still got five days to go," Summer said.

"Maybe we should plan for more than twenty customers," Campbell suggested. "Just in case."

"Good thinking." I opened my notebook and made a note to order extras of everything. "Can I see the list, Summer?"

"Sure." Summer handed me her notebook.

I was surprised to see my cousin Jeremy's name at the top of the list. In fact, half the reservations were from Harrington boys. Carter and Trevor had signed up, too!

Was Jeremy planning to play some kind of prank? Or did he really want to eat at Porter House? I had to find out. I ducked into the hall to use the phone and dialed Jeremy's room.

"Hi, Jeremy," I said. "I just noticed that you made a reservation for dinner at Porter House on Saturday."

"Yeah," Jeremy said. "I felt bad after Trevor and I kept changing our orders just to give you a hard time at the Burger Bistro. So I got a bunch of guys to make reservations."

Isn't that awesome, Diary? Sometimes my cousin can be totally cool.

"Thanks, Jeremy," I said. "You won't regret it. Brigitte's desserts are fabulous. And Ashley's Chunky Chicken Under Cover is the best!"

Phoebe raced down the stairs as I hung up.

"Where are you going in such a hurry?" I asked.

"To the printer with the menu," Phoebe said. She held up the sample menu for me to see.

"Wow!" I exclaimed. "This is great, Phoebe."

Phoebe had used parts of the article about the Chicago cooking contest my mother won. She put the headline at the top:

They Picked the Potpie!

Phoebe had also found an article about Brigitte's mom. She used that headline in the middle of the menu:

Jardin Pastries: The Perfect Ending!

She placed quotes from both articles in the spaces around our menu items. There was a blue ribbon in the lower corner.

"I've shown it to a few people," Phoebe said. "They like it. But I can't wait for everyone to approve it."

"Why not?" I asked.

"I have just enough time to get to the printer before he closes," Phoebe explained.

"Will the menus be done by Friday?" I asked.

"Only if I drop this off today," Phoebe explained. "We'll have to pay extra for a rush job if we wait until tomorrow."

"Then you'd better get going," I said. I was sure the

girls who hadn't seen the menu would love it. And paying for a rush job might put us over our budget.

Phoebe gave me the printer's price estimate and left.

The phone rang again and Summer ran to answer it. I went back into the lounge. Ashley came in right after me. The meeting had already started.

Elise was explaining her idea for the restaurant decor. "I thought it would be cool to combine our chicken food theme with Christmas. So I looked for chicken decorations online."

"Do they make chicken decorations?" Lexy asked.

"Not Christmas chickens." Elise laughed. "But they make chicken baskets. They'll look great with red ribbons, pinecones, and fake evergreen. We can call them Christmas Clucks."

"Elise is the only person I know who can make chickens cute and festive," Cheryl said.

"I've got two more reservations, Mary-Kate," Summer said. She stood by the door in case the phone rang again.

"How much will the decorations cost, Elise?" I asked.

"The baskets are on sale. I can get everything else at the discount store." Elise handed me a paper with the prices.

"Do you have a shopping list, Brigitte?" I asked.

"Not yet." Brigitte shrugged. "I haven't decided which dessert to make."

"Get your mom's recipe for the brownies, Brigitte," Ashley suggested. "The one I ate the other day was so good!"

"I like the Raspberry Snowdrop cookies," Summer said. The phone rang again. She went to answer it.

"I vote for those amazing éclairs," Jolene said.

"We don't have to vote. I've almost decided," Brigitte said. "I'll have a list of ingredients for you soon, Mary-Kate."

"No problem," I told her. I didn't want to seem pushy.

Ashley gave me her list of supplies this morning, Diary. Everything but one item. She finally told me why her Chunky Chicken Under Cover didn't taste as good as Mom's. My sister doesn't know the secret ingredient!

But Ashley is determined to find out what it is. So I'm not worried.

"Two more, Mary-Kate!" Summer ran in and waved her notebook. "That makes twenty-four reservations. We might have *thirty* by Saturday!"

That was a lot of extra people!

I sat down with my calculator to add everything up. Mrs. Pritchard had given us price lists from the market. We had to buy food and decorations. And I had to rent tables and chairs.

Uh-oh! *Big* problem!

Buying food for thirty customers will cost more than we're allowed to spend. Porter House will be over budget.

We can't win the five-star rating if we spend more money than we have! Will I lose my bet with Dana?

Dear Diary,

Okay, I admit it: Brigitte is starting to bug me. Every time I walk into a room, she walks out.

I didn't spoil Brigitte's practise recipe on purpose. I tried to apologise, but she wouldn't listen. I decided to try one more time after the restaurant staff meeting today.

I waited until Layne left before I walked up to Brigitte. I was glad Brigitte was getting to know my friends. And I didn't want everyone to know we were having a cooking feud.

"I'm sorry your recipe burned yesterday, Brigitte," I said. "Did whatever it was come out okay the second time?"

"Why are you so interested?" Brigitte asked. "Are you spying on me?"

"Why would I spy on you?"

"To find out what dessert I'm planning to make," Brigitte said.

"What difference would that make?" I asked. "We're on the same team, Brigitte. We should be helping each other."

"What makes you think I need help?" Brigitte huffed. Then she stomped out the door.

Something is really wrong here, Diary. The real Brigitte is nice and friendly. She's avoiding me for a reason. I just don't know what it is. But I'm going to find out.

But first I had to find the secret ingredient for my potpie.

I went to the computer center and signed on to the Internet. I didn't have Internet in my room. Then I did a search for potpie recipes.

I was just a little kid when I watched Mom make Chunky Chicken Under Cover. But I'm pretty sure the missing ingredient is something cooks use a lot. My mom said most cooks have the same herbs and spices she kept on her rack.

The potpie recipes I found online all used a combination of the same seasonings. They were the exact same seasonings I already knew about in my mom's recipe.

There was only one solution. I had to make something else. Thank goodness it wasn't too late to change my recipe!

Phoebe came into our room while I was looking through some cookbooks I checked out of the library. "I'm bummed I didn't see you this afternoon," she said.

"Why?" I said, looking up from the cookbook.

"I wanted to show you the menu," Phoebe said. "I used parts of the newspaper article about your mother and the Chicago cooking contest."

"You did?" *Oh, no!* I thought. "Can I see it?" I asked.

"Sure." Phoebe pulled a computer printout of her bag. "I got Brigitte's mom on it, too!"

The menu looked awesome. Phoebe had worked hard on it. I didn't want to hurt her feelings, but I had to tell Phoebe I had changed my mind about making Chunky Chicken Under Cover.

"I dropped it off at the printer's today," Phoebe said.

I gasped. "It's at the printer?"

"Yeah." Phoebe grinned. "The menus are being printed now. Elise went to shop for her decorating supplies. And Mary-Kate was going to call in orders before her meeting at the Burger Bistro."

Yikes! I thought. *The food and menus have been ordered! So I* have *to make Chunky Chicken Under Cover without the secret ingredient.* Oh, Diary, what am I going to do?

Chapter 7

Monday

Dear Diary,

Rhonda was going crazy when I got to the Burger Bistro. "Two waitresses called in sick with the flu!" she exclaimed.

"Is the volunteers' meeting cancelled?" I asked.

"I'm afraid so, Mary-Kate," Rhonda said. "I have to order the food for the holiday dinner tonight so it'll get here on time. But I have to wait tables, too."

"I can call in orders for you," I said. "Is everything written down?"

"Yes, I've got the forms all filled out." Rhonda looked relieved. "Thanks. That would be so great. Come on. You can use the phone in the office."

I can call in my Porter House food orders, too, I thought. I meant to do them at White Oak, but I ran out of time.

I followed Rhonda past the kitchen to the office. I sat down at the desk.

Rhonda handed me her order forms. "The phone numbers are on the forms."

"Okay." I glanced at the top form. Rhonda had filled in all the blanks. I knew the name of each item, how many to order, and the cost.

"Any questions?" Rhonda asked.

"No, I'll be fine." I smiled. And I went to work.

First I read Rhonda's whole grocery order. My eyes popped with surprise when I saw the price of a bag of rolls.

Rhonda's supplier charged *half* what our local grocery store charges for rolls!

I looked at Rhonda's other order. The Burger Bistro buys chicken from a butcher. That price is less than the grocery store's, too. And they deliver by the next day.

I did some quick calculations. If I ordered the dinner rolls and chicken from Rhonda's suppliers, Porter House wouldn't be over budget!

I wanted to pick up the phone and call Dana right away. I wanted to tell her that she'd be making my bed!

Tuesday

Dear Diary,

I hurried back to the dorm after classes today. I still had to rent tables and chairs for our restaurant. As I started up the stairs, I heard a shriek.

What's going on? I wondered. My heart was pounding.

The screams came from the kitchen. It sounded like Ashley! I raced down the hall and stopped in the kitchen doorway.

Feathers were floating around the room. Lavender Duncan and Alyssa Fuji stood by the counter, trying not to laugh.

Ashley held a chicken by the neck. The bird was covered in white feathers and still had its head and feet attached. I was so shocked, I could only stare.

Then the chicken's head flopped over, and Ashley shrieked again.

Dear Diary,

Mary-Kate stood in the kitchen doorway, staring.

"What's this?" I demanded. I held the chicken up higher. Its dangling feet swayed.

"A cheap chicken." Mary-Kate giggled.

A white feather fluttered to the floor. I dropped the limp bird onto the counter.

Lavender and Alyssa both burst out laughing.

"Come look," I said to Mary-Kate. I pointed. There were eight more chickens with feathers, heads, and feet in the crate on the floor.

Mary-Kate tried to explain. "When the butcher

said 'whole chickens,' I didn't know he meant whole as in *everything* still attached."

"What am I going to do with these?" I cried.

"First you have to cut the heads off," Alyssa said, giggling.

"*I'm* not cutting the heads off," I said.

Lavender grimaced. "I'd rather lose the restaurant contest than cut off chicken heads."

"Or ugly chicken feet." Alyssa shuddered.

"I'll be right back." Mary-Kate turned and left. She probably felt awful about the mistake. But that didn't solve my problem. I can't cook with chickens that look like they should still be on the farm! I knew feathers weren't my mom's secret ingredient!

Mary-Kate returned with Miss Viola.

"I see we have a problem," our housemother said.

"I ordered them from a butcher so we wouldn't go over budget," Mary-Kate explained. "I can't return them."

"Tell you what," Miss Viola said. "You girls pluck the feathers, and I'll cut up and bone the chickens."

"Yuck!" I cried.

"Come on, Ashley," Mary-Kate said. "It won't be that bad."

"If I'm doing it, so are you, Mary-Kate," I said to my sister.

"This is my fault," Mary-Kate said, "so I'll stay to help."

"Okay, then," I said. I felt a little calmer.

Lavender, Alyssa, Mary-Kate, and I sat on the kitchen floor. Miss Viola put a plastic bag down for the feathers. We each took a chicken out of the crate.

"Ewww." Lavender gripped her chicken around the neck. She tugged on a feather, but it wouldn't come out.

"You have to yank it," Miss Viola explained. She jerked a feather out and dropped it into the plastic bag.

"Taking them out one by one will take forever!" Alyssa said, grabbing a handful of feathers. Most of them came out when she pulled.

You know, Diary, I can't even describe how totally gross it is to yank feathers off dead chickens – especially with Miss Viola standing behind you whacking the birds into pieces!

"Why did the chicken cross the road?" Mary-Kate asked.

"I don't know," I said.

"Why did it?" Lavender asked.

"To escape Ashley's pot-hole-ders!" Mary-Kate giggled.

Alyssa frowned. "I don't get it."

"Roads are full of pot *holes*," Mary-Kate said. "And you use pot *holders* when you cook."

"Oh!" Alyssa grinned. "That is pretty funny."

"Okay, I've got one," Lavender said. She dropped a fistful of feathers into the bag. "What happens to chickens who can't spell?"

Everyone looked blank.

"They become fryers instead of fliers," Lavender said.

"Or they come home to roast instead of to roost," Mary-Kate said.

"With a cluck-cluck here" – I spoke the line from the children's song – "Old MacDonald Had a Farm."

"And a cluck-cluck there!" Alyssa sang.

Everyone started singing. "Here a cluck, there a cluck, everywhere a cluck-cluck!"

After we finished that song, we all cluck-clucked instead of singing the words to our favorite Top 40 hits. We laughed so hard, my stomach hurt!

Ashley looked at me and grinned. Then she said, "This is the first and last chicken-plucking party I'll ever go to!"

Chapter 8

Wednesday

Dear Diary,

Sometimes nothing runs smoothly no matter how hard you try. You won't believe what happened today.

MARY-KATE'S DIARY

I owed Ashley a huge favor after dumping whole, unplucked chickens on her, so I helped her put away the groceries.

Ashley checked off the items as the delivery guy brought them into the dorm kitchen.

I put the bags of salad greens and bottles of dressing in the refrigerator.

"The pastry squares and butter go in the refrigerator, too, Mary-Kate," Ashley said.

"Good thing the fridge is so big!" I stored everything neatly to make more room.

"Okay, let's see . . . " Ashley lined up the potpie ingredients on the table. "Onion, garlic, flour, mushrooms, and sage."

"Is that everything?" I asked.

"Everything except the rolls," the delivery guy said. He handed me three bags of rolls.

"Thanks!" I put the bags on the counter. There were twelve rolls in each bag. Thirty-six rolls – exactly what Ashley wanted.

I turned back around just as the deliveryman brought in several more bags of rolls. He put them on the counter.

"Those aren't ours," I said.

The delivery guy ignored me and left.

Ashley looked up from her clipboard. "Is something wrong, Mary-Kate?"

"No," I said. I knew I hadn't ordered this many rolls. The delivery guy would have to take them back.

Except the delivery guy carried in *more* bags of rolls. He dropped them on the stove.

"Wait!" I followed him. "There's been a mistake. I only ordered—"

"Thirty-six bags of rolls." The delivery guy showed me the order.

"No, that's not right," I protested. "I only wanted three bags!"

The delivery guy put several bags of rolls in my arms. Then he went back to his truck for more!

"Need some help?" Ashley asked.

"Yes! Tell that guy to take these rolls back!"

"Sir!" Ashley ran out the door, waving her pen. "I need to talk to you!"

I looked around for a place to put the bags I was holding. I didn't want to squash the rolls. I had to return them!

I found a bare spot on the table. I put the bags down and turned around as Ashley came back inside.

With more bags of rolls!

"He won't take them back," Ashley said. She dropped her bags. "Do something, Mary-Kate!" she pleaded. "I don't have room to cook!"

"I'll take care of it," I said. "As soon as I figure out what went wrong."

"Telephone for Mary-Kate!" Phoebe stuck her head in the door. She blinked when she saw the piles of rolls. "Omigosh. It looks like a bakery exploded! What are we going to do with all those rolls?"

"I'll fix it! I'll fix it!" I said as I rushed out of the kitchen. I picked up the phone in the hall. "Hello?"

"Hi, Mary-Kate. It's Rhonda. I've got a problem."

I doubted Rhonda's problem was as big as my problem. "What's the matter?" I asked.

"I wanted you to order thirty-six *bags* of rolls," Rhonda said. "I got thirty-six *rolls*! That's not nearly enough."

Now I knew what went wrong. The supplier had mixed up my order with the order for the Burger Bistro!

"Don't worry, Rhonda!" I almost laughed, I was so relieved. "I've got thirty-three bags of rolls you can have."

This could have been a disaster, Diary – for both the Porter House restaurant and Rhonda's holiday dinner.

I sure hope nothing else goes wrong.

Dear Diary,

I stayed in the kitchen to organise everything after the delivery truck drove away.

First I carefully stacked the bags of rolls on the floor in the lounge. Then I double-checked my potpie ingredients.

That's when I realised that all the cooking supplies were mine. Nothing had been delivered for Brigitte's desserts.

Does Mary-Kate know what Brigitte plans to make? I wondered. Our restaurant would be open for business Saturday night – in three days! I hoped it wasn't too late to order more ingredients.

I went upstairs to check my mother's handwritten recipe one more time. I still wanted to find the missing ingredient, but I was running out of ideas.

Brigitte's room is right across the hall from the room I share with Phoebe. Brigitte's door was open. I glanced inside and saw that her window was open, too. Homework papers were blowing all over the place!

I rushed into Brigitte's room to close the window. As I reached over the desk to push the window down, I saw a pink box with silver writing.

It was an official Monique Jardin pastry box.

And inside the box was an éclair.

Exactly like the éclairs Brigitte had brought to the cook-off!

Everyone had voted for Brigitte to be the Porter House chef.

Even me!

But Brigitte hadn't made the éclairs we all liked so much.

Her mother, the famous French chef, had baked them. I was sure of it. There was no way she could have made them exactly the same way.

Brigitte had cheated. And that explained everything.

Brigitte had been trying to cook something in the dining hall kitchen. She had blamed me for messing it up. But she had probably spoiled the recipe herself.

Brigitte hadn't picked a dessert to make, or given Mary-Kate a supply list, because she couldn't bake!

Maybe Brigitte had been avoiding me because she didn't want me to know she had cheated and lied.

But now I do know, Diary. I'm just not sure what to do about it. Or what it means for the Porter House restaurant.

Chapter 9

Thursday

Dear Diary,

This afternoon I helped Rhonda load the rolls into her car. Then I went back to the Burger Bistro with her. I sure didn't expect to find Dana Woletsky waiting for us!

"What are you doing here, Dana?" I asked.

"I'm writing a story about the holiday dinner for the school newspaper," Dana explained.

"And we appreciate the extra publicity, Dana," Rhonda said.

Dana looked at Rhonda. "What's Mary-Kate doing here?"

"She's helping me with the holiday dinner," Rhonda said. "I'm short of help because so many families want to come. The response is much better than we had imagined!"

"Just like us," I said. "Porter House has so many reservations, some people might have to eat standing up!"

"*That* won't impress Mr. Dupont," Dana said.

"I was just kidding." I rolled my eyes.

Dana bristled. "So does Phipps House."

"I'm glad we're all doing so well," Rhonda said.

I realized Rhonda didn't want us to argue. Dana took the hint and stopped bickering, too.

"The holiday dinner is very important to me," Rhonda went on. "It's a lucky thing Mary-Kate already knows how things work at the Burger Bistro. At least I can count on her. I could use ten more like you, Mary-Kate." Rhonda smiled. "I have to check the phone messages. Be right back."

Dana didn't say anything until Rhonda closed the office door. "So you're waiting on tables at Rhonda's holiday dinner? How does everyone at Porter House feel about that?"

"They know I can handle both jobs, Dana," I said. "It's no big deal."

Dana arched an eyebrow. "Gee, I think someone who can be in two places at once is a very big deal."

"What do you mean?" I asked.

"The holiday dinner is *Saturday*." Dana couldn't hide her glee. "The same night the restaurants are open for the White Oak Winter Festival."

I never thought to check the date, Diary! And every time Rhonda and I started talking about the details, something cut the conversation short.

This is a *huge* emergency.

I can't back out on Rhonda now. She doesn't have enough help, and I promised.

But I can't let Ashley and everyone else at Porter House down, either.

Oh, Diary, what am I going to do?

Dear Diary,

Finding the missing ingredient may be hopeless. I've looked through cookbooks. I even called a TV cooking show! But my mom's secret is still a secret.

I know my mother told me the secret ingredient, but I can't remember. And that just makes it more frustrating.

Sometimes if I stop thinking about a problem, the answer suddenly comes to me. I decided to try that. I went downstairs to watch TV.

I ran into Brigitte in the front hall. She had just come in the door with a package.

"Hi, Brigitte," I said. "Is that from your mother?"

"Maybe." Brigitte turned the package so I couldn't see the label. Then she hurried up the stairs.

Is that another box of pastries from Monique Jardin? I wondered. *Is Brigitte planning to pass them off as hers at our restaurant?*

I hate knowing Brigitte's secret, Diary. That makes *two* secrets that might hurt our dorm's chances of winning the five-star rating.

I really needed someone to talk to.

There was only one person I could trust completely. I found Mary-Kate. We went to the Student Union and sat on a sofa in the corner.

"What's wrong, Ashley?" Mary-Kate asked.

"I don't know where to start," I said. "I – "

Then Dana walked by and interrupted.

"Have you solved your split-personality problem, Mary-Kate?" Dana asked. "I like the covers of my bed tucked in perfectly. I just thought I should warn you."

I had no idea what Dana was talking about. And she left before I could ask. Mary-Kate looked worried.

"I've got a big problem, too, Ashley," Mary-Kate said. "I promised Rhonda I'd help with her holiday dinner for police officers and firefighters."

"What's wrong with that?" I asked.

"I just found out the dinner is on Saturday night," Mary-Kate explained. "The same night as our restaurant."

"That's a pretty big problem," I said.

Mary-Kate nodded. "I feel terrible. I can't be in two places at once. So I'll have to back out of working for Rhonda or working for Porter House."

I didn't see how Mary-Kate could work both jobs, either.

"At least you're not a cheat," I said.

"Who's cheating?" Mary-Kate looked confused.

I told Mary-Kate my theory about Brigitte's desserts. I started with the éclair I found. I ended with the package Brigitte got today.

"So she already cheated," Mary-Kate pointed out. "She used her mother's éclairs to get elected chef."

"Yes, but this is worse," I said. "It's not fair to serve desserts made by a world-famous chef."

Mary-Kate agreed. "Jerome Dupont would pick gourmet desserts to win the five-star rating."

I nodded. "I don't want to tattle on Brigitte."

"I don't want to win if it's not fair," Mary-Kate said.

"We may not have to worry about that," I said. "I still can't figure out Mom's secret ingredient."

Mary-Kate sighed. "And without the secret ingredient – "

"Mr. Dupont won't like Chunky Chicken Under Cover very much," I finished. "Do you remember anything Mom said about the recipe?"

"Let me think." Mary-Kate frowned. "I remember something about time. Something Mom said. Maybe the secret isn't an ingredient."

"What else could it be?" I asked.

"It could be an instruction," Mary-Kate said.

"Like how long she baked the potpie in the oven?"

"That's written down on the recipe," I said. "And it doesn't have a star."

"Maybe she waited a few minutes before she put the potpie in the oven," Mary-Kate suggested.

"Maybe," I said. Figuring out my mom's secret seemed impossible. I just wished I could ask her.

Chapter 10

Friday

Dear Diary,

There's just no way to solve my double-duty problem. I can be at the Burger Bistro to help Rhonda with the holiday dinner. Or I can wait tables at Porter House.

I can't do both.

So I'll have to break my word and let someone down.

But I needed more time to decide. So I went ice skating with Campbell at the rink White Oak shares with Harrington. My cousin Jeremy was there.

"Hey, Jeremy!" I waved and skated over. He was talking with Carter, Trevor, and Ross Lambert. Ross is Ashley's boyfriend. "What are you guys up to?"

"We're still trying to choose a community service project," Carter said.

"We've got it narrowed down to two things," Ross said.

"We could shovel snow off sidewalks," Jeremy explained. "Or serve out soup at the shelter."

"I want to teach old people how to play computer games," Trevor said. "My grandpa always wants me to explain stuff."

"We voted that idea down, Trevor." Jeremy

looked at me. "Break the tie for us, Mary-Kate. Shovels or soup?"

"I don't like either choice," Trevor said.

But I suddenly had a totally awesome idea. "What about something you haven't thought of?" I asked.

Dear Diary,

I spent all afternoon in the kitchen with Phoebe, Lavender, and Alyssa. We had a lot to do before our restaurant opened. Miss Viola supervised. But we did the work.

"Okay, Chef," Lavender said. "What do you want us to do?"

"You and Alyssa can rinse the salad greens," I said. "They'll stay fresh in the refrigerator."

"We're on it." Alyssa opened the refrigerator and pulled out bags of salad.

"Phoebe and I will chop vegetables while the chicken cooks," I said.

"Great!" Phoebe grinned. "I've had practise chopping."

"Chopping veggies is a lot easier than plucking feathers!" Alyssa joked.

"And cluck-clucking popular songs in two-part harmony," Lavender added.

"I can't squawk a tune to save myself," Phoebe teased.

I couldn't stop thinking about Brigitte.

Only Mary-Kate and I knew Brigitte had cheated to win the cook-off. Would Brigitte buy a dessert for the restaurant? Or use something her mother sent?

I filled two big pots with water and put them on the stove. Phoebe and I chopped garlic, onions, and mushrooms until the water boiled. Then we dropped the chicken parts into the pots.

"Eeeee!" Phoebe squealed as she held a chicken leg into the air for all of us to see.

"What's wrong?" I asked. My heart pounded.

"That leg still has a foot!" Phoebe pointed to it. The foot *was* still attached to the leg.

"Miss Viola must have missed that one," I said.

"Yuck. We can't use this one," unless the secret ingredient is chicken feet," I joked.

Lavender and Alyssa giggled. Soon, we were all laughing.

I was amazed at how much work we did in advance. The salad greens were washed and stored. The veggies were chopped. And the chicken was cooked and cubed. We'd just have to mix, roll, and bake tomorrow night.

"Good job, guys," I said. I dried off the last spoon and put it away. "That's all for today."

"Let's go see if Summer and Elise need help setting up the tables," Phoebe said.

"Sure," Lavender said. "I'd rather tie bows on fake chickens than yank feathers off real ones."

"I have something else to do first," I said.

Phoebe, Alyssa, and Lavender went to the lounge. I went upstairs. I took a deep breath and knocked on Brigitte's door.

"Just a mi-minute," Brigitte called out.

Her voice sounded shaky. When she opened the door I knew why. Brigitte's eyes were red. She had been crying.

"What is it, Ashley?" Brigitte blinked back a tear.

I wasn't annoyed anymore. I felt sorry for her.

"I, uh – I know why you're upset, Brigitte," I said. I was careful not to sound angry.

Brigitte sniffled and dabbed her nose with a tissue.

"I know your secret," I went on. "Do you . . . uh . . . want to talk about it?"

Brigitte started to cry. She stepped back so I could walk into her room. Then she closed the door and sat on her bed.

"I guess that means you know that I can't bake," Brigitte finally said.

"Yeah, I know." I could tell Brigitte felt terrible. I didn't want to make her feel worse.

"I – I didn't want to be in the cook-off," Brigitte stammered. "But everyone got so excited about the Raspberry Snowdrop cookies."

"They were really good cookies," I said.

"That was the first time I felt like I was . . . visible," Brigitte said. "No one had paid any attention to me before. Except you."

That wasn't true, but I didn't interrupt.

"Being the chef changed everything," Brigitte admitted. "I felt like I could fit in. And I did."

"Everyone wanted to be your friend," I said. "But not because they thought you could cook."

"Maybe." Brigitte blew her nose. "But now I've just messed up everything."

"No, you haven't," I said.

Brigitte didn't buy that. "Yes, I have. I thought I could learn to make *one* recipe. But I couldn't."

That was true, but I just listened patiently.

"So I let everyone think I had made my mother's éclairs." Brigitte glanced at the new package on her desk.

"What's in the package?" I asked.

"Raspberry-chocolate truffles from my mom," Brigitte said. "I thought about using them for the restaurant. But I'd feel too guilty."

"Yeah," I agreed. "We have to make our own stuff to win fair and square."

"That's why you should have won the cook-off." More tears rolled down Brigitte's cheek. "You've been so nice. And you're a great cook."

"Actually, I'm not such a great cook," I confessed. "I've been freaking out all week."

"Why?" Brigitte asked.

"Because I can't figure out the secret ingredient that makes my mom's potpie so special," I said.

"You were serious about that?" Brigitte looked surprised.

I nodded. "I was afraid *I'd* let everyone down."

"What are we going to do?" Brigitte sounded really upset. "Everyone's counting on us. And they've all worked so hard on the restaurant."

"We're even overbooked!" I said. "So we'll just have to do what we should have done all along."

Brigitte frowned, puzzled. "What's that?"

"Trust each other and help each other," I said. "Somehow, we'll make the Porter House restaurant a huge success."

I had one more question for Brigitte before I left. "What was that stuff that boiled over in the dining hall kitchen?"

"Caramel sauce," Brigitte said. "Burnt sugar smells gross."

"Totally!" We both laughed. I had my friend back.

Chapter 11

Saturday

Dear Diary,

Everyone in Porter House was so busy this afternoon.

Alyssa and Lavender rolled puff-pastry squares into flat crusts. Phoebe put the bottom crusts in baking dishes. I was getting ready to make the first batch of sauce.

Lexy, Campbell, and Layne came in. They all wore white shirts, black pants, and had red poinsettia corsages. They looked very festive for the White Oak Winter Festival.

"We're supposed to set up the salad station," Lexy said.

"With baskets for rolls," Campbell added.

"Put the bowls on the counter by the fridge," I said. "We'll fill them with salad greens right before you serve."

"Can we microwave the rolls?" Layne asked. She put a cloth napkin in each breadbasket.

"Absolutely," I said. "Warm rolls might get us some extra points with Mr. Dupont."

"Let's hope!" Campbell exclaimed.

"Are you ready to use the oven, Brigitte?" I called across the room.

"Almost!" Brigitte poured brownie batter into a shallow pan. Then she mixed in chocolate flakes and fresh raspberries.

"Those are going to taste super, Brigitte!" I grinned and put butter in a pan to melt.

Brigitte was using one of my basic brownie recipes. Adding chocolate flakes and raspberries was her idea. The brownies would be served with a dab of whipped cream and a trickle of chocolate sauce. They wouldn't be *exactly* like her mom's brownies. But we thought Mr. Dupont would be impressed.

"I sure hope these come out okay." Brigitte placed two pans of brownies in the oven.

"They will," I assured her. "The potpies will be ready to bake when the brownies are done." I added onions, garlic, and flour to the melted butter.

"I wish I could be more help." Brigitte pulled jars of spices off the shelf. She lined them up on the counter.

I ran my finger across the labels on the spice bottles. I was looking for sage.

"We're running out of time," Brigitte said.

I stopped moving my finger and looked up. My eyes widened. "What did you say?"

"We're running out of time?" Brigitte repeated.

"That's it!" I slapped my forehead.

"That's what?" Brigitte looked confused.

"Thyme!" I picked up the spice bottle marked THYME.

Brigitte frowned. She didn't understand.

I quickly explained. "Right before my mother put on the top crust, she always said, 'Now all we need is a little thyme.' Then she'd sprinkle a herb on top of the sauce. I thought she meant *time*! T-i-m-e."

"But she meant the seasoning!" Brigitte grinned. "Thyme is the secret ingredient!"

I was so thrilled, I could hardly talk! Thanks to Brigitte, my chicken potpies would have the secret ingredient.

They'd be exactly like my mom's potpies!

But would Jerome Dupont like Chunky Chicken Under Cover as much as the judges in Chicago did?

Dear Diary,

Rhonda wasn't too sure about my idea at first. But she finally agreed. It was the only way to solve her problem.

I stayed at the Burger Bistro just long enough to help set the tables. Then I raced back to Porter House. It was almost time for our restaurant to open.

I felt bad about missing the setup work. But I'd feel worse after I broke the bad news to my sister and friends.

"Where have you been, Mary-Kate?" Summer asked.

Summer looked relieved when I came in the front door. She also looked gorgeous in a sparkly white top, a black jacket, and matching black slacks.

"Our first customer will be here soon," Jolene said. She taped a menu on the wall outside the lounge door.

Everyone else was taking a short break in the lounge.

"We're ready," Kristen said. "The brownies are cooling. And the potpies are in the oven. But you still have to change, Mary-Kate."

"I know, but – " I hesitated. But there's only one way to break bad news. I blurted it out. "We lost ten reservations."

"What?" all the girls exclaimed.

"What do you mean?" Ashley asked.

"Well, I volunteered to work at the holiday dinner," I said. "Except I didn't know it was tonight!"

"You have to be *here,* Mary-Kate," Layne said. "You're the only one who has experience waiting on tables."

"I'll be here," I said. "But Jeremy and his friends won't."

"Is this one of Jeremy's pranks?" Ashley asked.

"No," I assured her. "The boys needed a community service project. So they're going to work Rhonda's holiday dinner in my place."

"So Rhonda has all the volunteers she needs, and we have Mary-Kate," Ashley said.

"And we still have twenty reservations," I pointed out.

"Let's hope no one else cancels," Summer said. She looked a little nervous. "We need at least twenty."

"We've got another problem," Ashley said. "We made food for *thirty* people! We'll have leftovers."

"Mrs. Pritchard will lower our grade if we waste food," Phoebe added.

Uh-oh. I hadn't thought about that.

"Wait! The extra food won't be wasted if we donate it to the Burger Bistro as a meal for the volunteers," I said.

"Now *that's* a great idea!" Campbell exclaimed.

Everyone else agreed. All our problems were solved.

"And just think, Mary-Kate," Ashley said. "It only took ten boys to replace one you."

Chapter 12

Saturday

Dear Diary,

This was it. The make-or-break-it time had arrived. I took the potpies out of the oven. Layne and Campbell took salads and rolls to the first customers.

"Just in time," I said. "And I don't mean t-h-y-m-e."

Brigitte giggled. "The potpies look perfect, Ashley."

They did look good. The crusts were golden brown. But would they taste as fantastic as my mom's Chunky Chicken Under Cover? I couldn't sample it before we had to serve it.

"This isn't fair, Brigitte." Phoebe pretended to pout. "You have to let us taste-test your brownies."

"What do you think, Ashley?" Brigitte asked.

"One bite," I said. "For everyone in the kitchen."

Phoebe grinned and handed Brigitte a cake cutter.

I sampled the brownies, too. I couldn't believe it, Diary. They were nearly as good as the brownies Brigitte's mother had sent from France!

Mary-Kate raced into the kitchen. She was

wearing her waitress uniform and poinsettia corsage. "Jerome Dupont is coming in the front door!" she said in a loud whisper.

My stomach flip-flopped.

"Here we go." Brigitte squeezed my hand.

"I was elected to wait on him," Mary-Kate said. "I hope I don't drop anything in his lap!"

"Please, don't!" I joked. But I was nervous, too. We only had one chance to impress him. "You'll be fine, Mary-Kate."

Mary-Kate nodded and left.

Brigitte volunteered to stay with Phoebe in the kitchen. That way I could watch what happened in the lounge dining room. I promised to report back.

I peeked into the hall. A large man walked in the front door and smiled at Summer. He was wearing a dark suit with a vest and a red tie. His hair was dark. And he had a moustache.

So that's Jerome Dupont, I thought.

"Right this way, Mr. Dupont," Summer said. She picked up a menu and walked into the lounge.

I walked to the lounge doorway and looked inside.

The tables looked fabulous with red tablecloths and green napkins. The chicken baskets sat on nests of fake evergreen in the middle of the tables. Red bows were tied around the chickens' necks. The effect was simple but elegant.

A White Oak math teacher and his wife were sitting at one table. Three senior girls were sitting at another table. Summer sat Mr. Dupont at the table by the fireplace.

"Thank you," Mr. Dupont said as he sat down. He took the menu and chuckled. "Chicken decorations and chicken potpie. Very clever."

Elise was standing on the far side of the lounge. She grinned from ear to ear.

Mary-Kate waited until Mr. Dupont put his napkin in his lap. Then she poured water into his glass.

"Would you care for something to drink, Mr. Dupont?" Mary-Kate asked. "We have cola, ginger ale, or iced tea."

"Water is fine," Mr. Dupont said. "I have a few other restaurants to visit this evening."

"Yes, sir," Mary-Kate said.

"So I'll skip the salad and roll and have your blue-ribbon potpie immediately." Mr. Dupont handed the menu back to Mary-Kate and took a sip of water.

"Yes, sir." Mary-Kate smiled and left. She paused as she went by me. "Did I do okay?" she asked.

"You were great," I whispered.

"Do you want to get the potpie ready for Mr. Dupont, Ashley?" Mary-Kate asked.

I shook my head. "No, Brigitte can handle it."

It seemed like forever before Mary-Kate came back with Mr. Dupont's Chunky Chicken Under Cover. Steam rose through the slits in the crust. It was hot from the oven.

Brigitte followed Mary-Kate and stopped beside me. "I wanted to see how much Mr. Dupont likes your potpie," she whispered.

We both tensed as Mary-Kate put the potpie on the table. Then she moved back to wait in the doorway with us.

Mr. Dupont breathed in the savory aroma. He nodded, but he didn't smile. He took a sip of water.

"He's washing other tastes out of his mouth," Brigitte explained. "It's called 'cleansing the palate.'"

My stomach churned when Mr. Dupont pushed his fork through the crust. I held my breath when he took a bite.

Mr. Dupont chewed and swallowed. He hesitated for a second. Then he exclaimed, "This is great!"

"Great!" I looked at Brigitte. "Is that good?"

Brigitte shrugged. "I don't speak American gourmet."

"I'm pretty sure that means it's very good," Mary-Kate said.

Mr. Dupont took another bite, and another. Then he put his fork down. "I'm sorry I have to stop. This is the best chicken potpie I've ever had."

Mary-Kate grinned.

Summer gave me a big thumbs-up.

Mr. Dupont ate two more bites of my potpie. Then he pushed the plate aside. Mary-Kate hurried over to the table.

"I'm ready for dessert," Mr. Dupont said. "And I'd like to meet Mademoiselle Jardin."

"He wants to meet *me*?" Brigitte whispered. She turned and ran back toward the kitchen.

Oh, no! I thought. *Brigitte is too shy to talk to Mr. Dupont!*

I turned and ran after Brigitte. She was in the kitchen, fixing a dessert brownie.

"Is that for Mr. Dupont, Brigitte?" I asked.

"Yes," Brigitte said. "I want it to be exactly right."

"It looks wonderful," I said.

"Good chefs always fix the plates when they serve someone important," Brigitte said. "My mother does it all the time."

I was so relieved! Brigitte just wanted everything to be perfect for Mr. Dupont.

Mary-Kate came in. She carried the plate of uneaten potpie.

"Why didn't Mr. Dupont finish the potpie?" Phoebe asked. "Didn't he like it?"

"He loved it!" Brigitte exclaimed.

"But he has to try dinners and desserts at *three* dorm restaurants tonight," Mary-Kate said. "He'll get too full if he eats everything."

"That makes sense," Phoebe said.

Brigitte picked up the dessert dish. The brownie was topped with whipped cream and chocolate syrup, like we'd planned. Then Brigitte added two raspberries as a garnish. Now it looked like a gourmet treat.

"I'm not sure *I* should take this," Brigitte said.

"I'm sure, Brigitte," I said. "Your brownies are fantastic. You should get the compliments."

Mary-Kate and I followed Brigitte down the hall. We waited in the doorway as she took the dish to Mr. Dupont's table.

"Bonsoir, Monsieur Dupont," Brigitte said. She set the dessert dish on the table.

I was pretty sure Brigitte had spoken French because she was nervous. But Mr. Dupont must have liked it. He answered her in French.

"Ceci semble magnifique," Mr. Dupont said. He picked up his fork. *"Que s'appelle-t-il?"*

I don't know a lot of French, Diary. But Mr. Dupont thought Brigitte's dessert looked magnificent. He wanted to know what it was called.

"Plaisir de framboise-chocolat," Brigitte said, and grinned. In English that means Chocolate-Raspberry Delight. Then Brigitte asked Mr. Dupont to enjoy it. *"Bon appetit, s'il vous plait."* she smiled.

"Merci." Mr. Dupont took a sip of water before eating a small bite of brownie.

Brigitte tensed. But I could tell she was more confident than when she first arrived at White Oak. She may have faked being able to cook, but she had made real friends over the past week.

Mr. Dupont's eyes lit up. *"Fantastique!"*

Brigitte beamed and hurried back into the hall. "He liked it!" Her face was flushed with happiness. "That is so great!" I was so happy for Brigitte.

"You did it!" Brigitte said, hugging me.

"*We* did it," I said. "I wouldn't have found the secret ingredient without you."

"And I wouldn't have learned to bake brownies without you!" Brigitte laughed. "We make a great team."

Brigitte and I are a great team, Diary. But now we're even better friends.

Sunday

Dear Diary,

"What's taking Campbell so long?" Ashley asked. She looked out the window. Then she paced back to the door.

Ashley, Phoebe, and Brigitte came to my room first thing this morning. Campbell had volunteered to get the Sunday morning newspaper.

We were all anxious to find out which dorm had won Jerome Dupont's five-star rating. A photographer from the *Gazette* had taken group pictures last night—at all the First Form dorms.

Finally Campbell burst through the door. She waved the newspaper. "We won!" Campbell said, laughing. "Porter House won!"

Ashley took the paper. The headline read:

Perfect Potpie Wins Again!

The picture of the Porter House restaurant staff was below the headline. There was also a smaller picture of Phoebe's fantastic menu.

"This is so cool!" Phoebe said, grinning. "We have our picture in a real newspaper!"

"There's also an article about Rhonda's holiday dinner for the police officers and firefighters," Campbell said. "That was a huge success, too. Everyone loved the gentlemen waiters!"

That made me smile. Jeremy was a joker, but he always came through for a good cause.

"So what are we going to do to celebrate?" Phoebe asked.

"We won a pizza party," Campbell reminded us.

"But that's not until tonight," Phoebe said.

"We can have an appetizer now," Brigitte said. "I have a whole box of Monique Jardin pastry treats in my room!"

"That's the best idea you've had since yesterday, Brigitte," Ashley said.

Everyone followed Brigitte into the hall.

I was the last one out of the room. I looked back at my unmade bed. First I was going to stuff myself with French pastry. Then I had an extra five-star bonus to collect.

Dana lost our bet. She had to make my bed this morning. And every day for the next week!

Ashley stopped when everyone else went upstairs. She waved as I closed the door. "Come on, Mary-Kate! I can't start celebrating without you."

My sister and I had worked hard to make the Porter House restaurant a success. We had solved problems, and Ashley had figured out the secret ingredient for our mom's prizewinning potpie. But, best of all, we had had a whole bunch of chicken-plucking fun.

"Coming, Ashley," I said, grinning. "Cluck-cluck-cluck!"

PSST! Take a sneak peek at

39 Candles, Cake, Celebrate!

Dear Diary,

I love surprises. Surprise parties, surprise phone calls from friends, sometimes even the meat loaf surprise in the school dining room. But surprises don't mean a thing to my sister. That's because no matter how hard I try, Mary-Kate just can't be surprised!

But this morning at breakfast, I decided to give it another shot.

"Hi, guys!" I said. I sat down at our usual table in the dining room. "How's the banana-nut oatmeal?"

"Let's just say you'll need a fork," Mary-Kate said as she poked at her bowl. "It's extra lumpy today!"

Oatmeal for breakfast is a big tradition here at the White Oak Academy for Girls in New Hampshire. It's hard to believe that our boarding school has been around for more than a hundred years. Maybe that's why our dining room looks like the inside of an old castle!

I glanced around the table at our friends. Cheryl Miller, Summer Sorensen, Phoebe Cahill, and Elise Van Hook all looked half-asleep as they swirled their spoons in their oatmeal.

"I'm still zonked out from that statewide history test we studied for all weekend," Cheryl said with a half-yawn.

"I'm just glad it's over." My roommate Phoebe groaned as she buttered her toast. "All those names to remember!"

Phoebe was wearing a denim miniskirt, purple cowboy boots, and tights with a black-and-white pattern that made me dizzy. Phoebe's way-cool clothes are all vintage. Sometimes I tease her that "vintage" is just a fancy word for hand-me-down!

"And all those dates! Like 1492, 1776, 1812!" Elise said. "I am so horrible at remembering dates!"

"Unless they're with Peter Juarez!" Mary-Kate teased.

Elise lowered her eyes and blushed. Peter is her boyfriend at the Harrington Academy for Boys, right down the road from our school.

All this talk about history tests and boys was distracting me from my plan. If I was going to start surprising Mary-Kate, I was going to have to start now. . . .

"Mary-Kate, forget about your lumpy banana-nut oatmeal," I declared. "Because this is your lucky day!"

"Why?" Mary-Kate asked. She glanced back at the kitchen. "Are there banana-nut muffins instead?"

I shook my head and said, "Something better. I have a surprise for you!"

"I love surprises!" Summer said. Her smile gleamed white against her California tan. "What is it, Ashley?"

"Summer!" Cheryl said. She rolled her dark eyes. "It wouldn't be a surprise if she said what it was."

"What do you think it is, Mary-Kate?" I asked. "Go ahead. Guess."

"Hmm," Mary-Kate said. She pressed her lips together and narrowed her eyes as she thought.

I held my breath.

Mary-Kate doesn't seem to have a clue! I thought. *Could this be it? Is she about to be surprised for the first time in our lives?*

"Let's see," Mary-Kate said slowly. Her blue eyes lit up, and she snapped her fingers. "Is it a peanut butter-chocolate energy bar with vanilla-yogurt icing?"

My jaw dropped. She did it again! Mary-Kate guessed another surprise!

"Well?" Mary-Kate asked with a smirk. "Is it?"

All eyes were on me as I pulled a peanut butter-chocolate energy bar with vanilla-yogurt icing from my bag. I tossed it on the table, saying, "You got it."

Our friends went totally wild.

"No way!" Elise squealed.

"How did you know that, Mary-Kate?" Phoebe asked.

Mary-Kate tore open the energy bar and took a bite. "Because I saw it in Ashley's bag yesterday," she said between chews.

"You saw it in my bag?" I asked, disappointed.

Summer clapped her hands and squealed, "Mary-Kate has X-ray vision, everybody. Just like Superman!"

"I don't have X-ray vision, Summer," Mary-Kate said. "Ashley was carrying her light blue jelly bag yesterday, and I could see right into it."

I gulped. Mary-Kate was right. My light blue jelly bag is practically transparent!

"Plus, Ashley hates yogurt icing on anything," Mary-Kate went on. "So I figured it must be for me."

I shook my head and said, "I should have known you can never be surprised. What was I thinking?"

BBC
ONLY £1.30
EXCLUSIVE:
Mary-Kate and Ashley's style secrets!
Girl TALK
Where Girls Get Together!
Take the ultimate friendship challenge!
Best Friends:
Cousin Nicky, the troublemaker!
6 Simple hairstyles to suit you
INSIDE your cringiest moments!
Don't miss! Star School
£1.30
If your free gift is missing, please ask your newsagent. Sorry, this gift is not available overseas.
Summer skirts for every girl
Plus Girl Band, Star Wars, Sleepover and cool competitions
25 May - 7 June 2003
ISSUE 271
Stars Gossip Friendship

Fundraising Frenzy

is written by first-time author, **Kirsten MacInnes**,
winner of Girl Talk's Mary-Kate and Ashley
short story competition

"We've GOT to raise that money!" Ashley cried, jumping up and down excitedly.

"Wow, Ashley! If you bounce around any more, people are going to start thinking that I have a kangaroo for a sister!" Mary-Kate laughed. The girls were walking to their first class of the day at White Oak Academy. Morning announcements had just ended. Ashley was so happy about the new library announcement that Mary-Kate was starting to wonder if her sister had springs at the bottom of her shoes.

"I know you really love to read Ashley, but why are you this excited about a new wing for the school library?" asked Mary-Kate. "White Oak already has an awesome library."

"It's not the library part I'm excited about, even though I think it will be great," Ashley explained. "I'm excited about what Mrs Pritchard said at the end of the announcement: Whoever raises the most money for the new wing will get to meet Verity Daniels!"

"I'm sorry, Ash," Mary-Kate said, looking confused. "I still don't get why this is such a big deal."

"Mary-Kate! Verity Daniels is only my favourite writer in the whole world!" Ashley exclaimed.

"Oh!" Mary-Kate said, finally remembering how much her sister loved Verity Daniels. "Right! You have every single book she's ever written! Well, that settles it. We definitely have to raise the most money."

"Thanks, Mary-Kate. I knew I could count on you," Ashley gave her sister a big hug. "Now we just have to figure out how we're going to do it!"

"How are we going to do that anyway?" asked Mary-Kate. Ashley took out her blue note book as well as her gold fountain pen.

"Maybe we could do something that we like to do," suggested Mary-Kate.

"Well, we love shopping and cool clothes so maybe we could use that and do something with it?" suggested Ashley.

"I have a brilliant idea that's beyond brilliant!"

cried Mary-Kate. "We could design, make and sell clothes and accessories!" Mary-Kate smiled.

"What a great idea!" said Ashley. "We can get old clothes and materials from the attic that we don't use any more!" They said. They both got to work as quickly as possible. They followed some sketches carefully and completed a couple of outfits. It was their last night and time was running out! "Oh no!" shrieked Ashley. "We don't have a lot of outfits and the announcement is tomorrow!"

Mary-Kate sighed. She didn't like to see her sister like this. She felt guilty. Maybe she should have worked faster or maybe she should have got more people to help. Ashley decided to take a nap upstairs. Meanwhile, Mary-Kate was going to face the risks. So without a whisper Mary-Kate slipped into the garage. She took out her small sewing box and set to work. She made an outfit with a cool top with ribbons coming out and a mini denim skirt with a pair of funky flip-flops with petals on them.

"This is for you Ashley!" thought Mary-Kate with renewed hope. After she had completed her masterpiece she went outside and put them up for sale. People started queuing up. She was officially in business. At the end Mary-Kate started to count up the money and ended up with over $800! The next day the announcement was going to be made. Ashley looked down at her toes full of disappointment. Mrs. Pritchard took out a small brown envelope.

"And the winners are... Mary-Kate and Ashley!" Ashley's face had lit up and she gave her sister a big hug.

"Well," said Ashley, "we better get packed, 'coz we have got a writer to meet!"

mary-kateandashley

	Title	ISBN
(1)	It's a Twin Thing	(0 00 714480 6)
(2)	How to Flunk Your First Date	(0 00 714479 2)
(3)	The Sleepover Secret	(0 00 714478 4)
(4)	One Twin Too Many	(0 00 714477 6)
(5)	To Snoop or Not to Snoop	(0 00 714476 8)
(6)	My Sister the Supermodel	(0 00 714475 X)
(7)	Two's a Crowd	(0 00 714474 1)
(8)	Let's Party	(0 00 714473 3)
(9)	Calling All Boys	(0 00 714472 5)
(10)	Winner Take All	(0 00 714471 7)
(11)	PS Wish You Were Here	(0 00 714470 9)
(12)	The Cool Club	(0 00 714469 5)
(13)	War of the Wardrobes	(0 00 714468 7)
(14)	Bye-Bye Boyfriend	(0 00 714467 9)
(15)	It's Snow Problem	(0 00 714466 0)

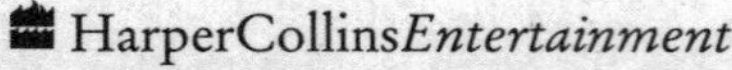

mary-kateandashley

(16)	Likes Me, Likes Me Not	(0 00 714465 2)
(17)	Shore Thing	(0 00 714464 4)
(18)	Two for the Road	(0 00 714463 6)
(19)	Surprise, Surprise!	(0 00 714462 8)
(20)	Sealed with a Kiss	(0 00 714461 X)
(21)	Now you see him, Now you don't	(0 00 714446 6)
(22)	April Fool's Rules	(0 00 714460 1)
(23)	Island Girls	(0 00 714445 8)
(24)	Surf Sand and Secrets	(0 00 714459 8)
(25)	Closer Than Ever	(0 00 715881 5)
(26)	The Perfect Gift	(0 00 715882 3)
(27)	The Facts About Flirting	(0 00 715883 1)
(28)	The Dream Date Debate	(0 00 715854 X)
(29)	Love-Set-Match	(0 00 715885 8)
(30)	Making a Splash	(0 00 715886 6)

HarperCollins*Entertainment*